# BURIED CURSES

by

Matthew Barron

*For Emma!! Thank you for tearing out the silver bones to save me from that werewolf!!*

*— MB*
*ARCHON 10/13/2*

Copyright 2021 by Matthew Barron. All rights reserved. No part of this book may be used or reproduced in any manner whatsoever without written permission except in the case of brief quotations embodied in critical articles and reviews. This is a work of fiction. All incidents and characters are fictitious. Any resemblance to real events or persons, living or dead, is purely coincidental.

Published by
Submatter Press

ISBN: 0-9850388-8-8
ISBN13: 978-0-9850388-8-5

For more information, to contact the author, or to order additional books, visit: submatterpress.com

A huge thank you to Lieutenant Colonel (Ret.) Hal Johnston for his invaluable guidance on military structure and ranks.

And also to Fritz and Susan Lantzer who helped me get into Jack's head by taking me to the firing range and letting me shoot their pistols.

This book is much more authentic thanks to their assistance.

# CHAPTER 1

My former sergeant, Anderson, leaned back in his chair with one leg propped on the conference table as he sipped my boss' bourbon. Cigar smoke puffed from his mouth when he spoke. "I knew you'd be back, Jackie. You could never turn away from a friend in need." He ran a hand over his crew cut. "I like the hair, by the way. Maybe I should try that."

Anderson's civilian suit jacket hung open, but his blond hair was still buzzed in military style. I kept my hair tied back into a shoulder length ponytail. Some said it emphasized the expanding bald spot on top of my head, but I wasn't in the military anymore and I'd be damned before I shaved it again.

Other than a slightly thicker neck and the civilian clothes, Anderson looked like he had stepped right out of my past into this office. After my last case, I almost expected to wake up from another nightmare, but the thick stench of bourbon and cigar smoke couldn't be simulated. This was really him.

My fists clenched so tightly, I thought my fingernails were going to cut the palms of my hands. "You aren't my friend." I couldn't believe how far my mood had tanked in the last few minutes. I had been on top of the world after completing the freakiest case of my short career and assumed that was the reason my boss was so cheerful with me, but Luis already had a new fish on my hook.

Anderson was the reason I had gotten kicked out of the Army. Everything bad that had happened to me over the last eleven years could be traced back to Anderson, and Luis expected me to help him!

Luis put a hand on my back and pulled out a chair. My boss, Luis Navarro, stood a full head shorter than me but was broad-shouldered. He didn't work the field much anymore, but he was still solid. "Have a seat, Jack. Let's hear what he has to say." Luis turned to Anderson across the table as we sat down. "Tell us your story, Mr. Anderson. What can we do to help you?"

Anderson brought his foot off the table and sat up in his chair. "I already explained—"

"For Jack's benefit," Luis added.

Anderson smiled and nodded at me. "Oh, yeah. Of course. It's simple. The FBI says I used my position in Iraq to ship stolen antiquities back to the States."

I raised my eyebrows at what Anderson considered *simple*. "Did you do it?"

Anderson scrunched his face. "Of course not! I would never do that."

"Not if you thought you'd get caught."

"Come on, Jackie," Anderson said. "I'm not the stupid guy I was back when we served together." He cast a concerned glance at Luis.

"Luis knows," I said. "Everything." I'd been forced to tell Luis about my service record and what had really happened in Afghanistan. It hadn't been Luis' choice to take me on board, but once we had made our arrangement, he vouched for me so I could get my PI License.

Anderson flopped his hands on the table in front of him. "I thought I was doing what was right, Jackie. Those insurgents might have had information."

"They were old men and kids!"

"That doesn't make them innocent."

"Our job was to guard them, not play games with them! Not torture them!"

"I had my orders too— to keep them awake and off balance. We did that! I made mistakes, but no one got seriously hurt on my watch— not like those places in Iraq."

"Not being as bad doesn't make it ok."

"You think my superiors didn't know what we were doing? Do you think Captain Braxton didn't know? Hell, I got commendations for how I ran that detention center! Look, I made mistakes. I pushed our games a little too far and didn't monitor the troops as well as I should. I didn't hear any objections from you at the time, Jackie."

"You were my superior officer! I never participated!"

"But you never objected, either. And you were the only one to get your photo taken."

I felt my face flush. The entire country had seen that stupid photo of me pointing at a row of naked, hooded prisoners. After eleven years, no one talked about it. If no one talked about it, I could pretend it had never happened, yet here was Anderson throwing it in my face.

"I was young and stupid, Jackie! None of us knew what we were doing out there. We were thrown into a situation and given power we didn't know how to manage. No one else could understand because they weren't there. No one else could appreciate the pressure we were under, or the lack of training. We shouldn't suffer the rest of our lives for that mistake."

Luis raised a hand and pushed downward, as though the action would depress the anger in my gut. "Mr. Anderson, you can see my colleague has some reservations about taking your case."

*Reservations* was putting it mildly.

Anderson wrote a number on a piece of paper and handed it to Luis. I didn't bother to look at it, but Luis sat up straight in his chair. Neither of us had experience with a case like this, but once Luis got dollar signs in his eyes, there was no talking him out of a job. That's how he'd gotten where he was in life. If you needed a PI in Albuquerque, you went to Luis Navarro first. He spent more time farming work to other investigators than doing anything himself these days, and he took a percentage of it all.

"Expenses would be extra," Luis said.

I shook my head. "Luis has plenty of investigators more experienced than me who can help you."

Anderson placed both palms flat on the table and stared into me. "I need you, Jackie. Why do you think I came all the way down here? You're the only person I trust."

"The only person you think you can manipulate. I'm not the same stupid kid I was back then, either!"

"Of course not, Jackie! I've never forgotten what you did for me. It made sense at the time for you to take the fall, but you could have turned on me. They already had the photo and you were a smaller target. I really thought if we kept my name out of the mud, I'd be able to keep you out of any real harm and once I got my promotion, I'd carry you up the ranks with me. We'd all come out okay."

"But if you couldn't, it didn't matter."

"When I became a civilian contractor, who do you think was the first person I wanted by my side? We could have made up for all the time you lost, but you'd disappeared. I couldn't find any trace of you until you popped up as a PI in Albuquerque."

I finally locked eyes with him. "It's *Jack,* not *Jackie!*"

If he knew I'd been gone all those years, it was possible he really had tried to look me up. I'd been as far off the grid as a person could get for nine years. I never would have taken a job with him, of course. Fringe science cults and homelessness were still preferable to working with Anderson again, but it was nice to know he'd at least thought of the life he'd ruined.

"What if the information we collect reveals you are guilty?" I asked. "I'm not hiding anything. I'm not covering for you again."

Luis attempted to interrupt. "Private Investigators don't determine innocence or guilt. Our job is to collect evidence."

Anderson shook his head. "I'm not asking you to cover for me, Jack. I just want the truth to come out."

"About everything?"

The corner of Anderson's mouth raised in a half-smile. "Everything about the stolen artifacts."

Luis smiled and nodded before I could object. "Great! It's settled. I'll get your lawyer on conference call and have her fax over the contracts."

"Contracts," I repeated. "Shit. We aren't working for Anderson. We're working for his lawyer."

Luis nodded. "Of course."

"So we'll have attorney-client privilege." I shook my head. "We're harboring a fugitive right now, aren't we?"

Anderson sipped his bourbon. "Don't worry, Jackie…" He quickly corrected himself, "Jack. Once the paperwork is settled, I'll turn myself in. I'll be out of your hair until this is all done."

I gritted my teeth. It also meant we wouldn't be legally obligated to release any information implicating Anderson in the crime. Obligated or not, I'd lose my job and my PI license before I'd keep quiet for him again.

While Luis handled the contracts, I stepped out of the smoky conference room for some air. Diane sat at the front desk with a Bluetooth phone receiver in her ear. Close-cropped black hair hugged her scalp and tapered against her sinewy, brown neck. Tiny red earrings provided a splash of color. When she heard the conference room door open, she turned her face away from the lists of numbers on her computer screen.

She took the receiver out of her ear and looked up at me with big, concerned eyes. "So, you're taking Anderson's case?"

"You heard?" I asked.

"You weren't exactly whispering in there."

I felt my face get warm. I didn't like losing my cool, and I definitely didn't like losing my cool in front of Diane. Other than my dogs, she was probably my best friend, the closest thing I had to family in this town and one of the few people whose opinion really mattered to me. I assumed she knew everything Luis did about why I had gotten kicked out of the military, but we'd never talked about it. I didn't want to ask if she'd seen that damning photo of me.

I no longer recognized the kid in that photo. When I saw it today, I could pretend it was someone else. I don't even remember why that unlit cigarette hung from my lips. I'd never smoked. I guess I had wanted to be considered one of the gang. I felt so ashamed that I had once considered those idiots' opinions so important.

Someone popped out with a camera, I cocked my thumb like a gun, pointed, and six months later I was infamous. I never would have done it if the prisoners hadn't been hooded. I couldn't have faced their eyes. I'd spent months before that avoiding the prison cells as much as possible, pretending the abuse wasn't as bad as it seemed, only to have my entire life defined by the fraction of a second it takes for a camera shutter to open and close.

I went over the meeting with Anderson in my mind and questioned how I had ended up agreeing to take this case. "You think I'm making a mistake?"

Diane shrugged. "Not necessarily. It could be a chance to confront some old demons. It's going to be difficult to remain emotionally detached though."

I raised my eyebrows and let my chest deflate. "You can say that again. I just want to prove him guilty as quickly as possible and put this behind me."

Diane chuckled. "Aren't you supposed to be working *for* him?"

I couldn't help but smile when she laughed.

Luis beamed at me when he emerged from the conference room and put a gentle hand on my shoulder. "Good job, Jack! We fly to Norfolk tomorrow afternoon!"

"Tomorrow?" I exclaimed. "I've got unfinished business here! There's no way I can settle everything before tomorrow!"

"Case is already getting cold!" Luis winked at Diane. "I'm sure Diane will take care of your dog."

Diane and I exchanged a glance. She and her son often watched the two dogs, but she did it out of friendship. It wasn't part of her office manager job. Luis was the only person in the company over her, and it felt like he was giving her an order, like she was now *obligated* to do this wonderfully generous thing she had been doing for me out of pure kindness. It felt even more inappropriate because I knew the two of them had been on at least one date. The invisible boundary between work and personal life had already been crossed. My stomach twisted in a knot. I'd finally found some semblance of stability here, but now our relationship dynamics were all out of whack and out of my control.

"Are we even licensed to work outside of New Mexico?" I asked.

"I'm licensed in a few states," Luis said, "but not Virginia. We'll be considered consultants only. In the unlikely event we need to follow someone or something, I've got a friend in state who will help us out."

"A friend?" I said.

Diane cocked her head. "I told you it pays to go to those trade shows and conferences, Jack."

I let out a long, resigned sigh. "I guess you have an answer for everything."

Luis smiled. "If this works out, maybe I'll franchise out, open an office on the east coast."

I couldn't tell if Luis was joking or not. It sounded preposterous, but I'm sure when he had first started working as a PI, it sounded absurd to say he would one day own the largest agency in New Mexico.

Anderson talked during the entire drive to the federal courthouse, a mindless series of inane, meaningless banter. He drank and laughed as though he were going to a party and not turning himself in to authorities. I stopped listening and dwelled on my own thoughts. Had the younger me been interested in such banality? Had I found it charming or charismatic? He had been the Sergeant, the life of the party, and I had wanted so much for him to like me.

At least Luis didn't let him smoke in the car. He knew how much that would bother me. Even though Luis thought my sensitive nose was an OCD figment of my imagination, he humored me today because my presence was important to Anderson, and Anderson was the money.

At last Luis pulled to the curb and put on the blinkers. We escorted Anderson past a large metal sculpture of the scales of justice. The information we gathered could tip those scales one way or another.

Anderson's lawyer had called ahead, and a federal marshal in a black polo shirt waited next to the metal detector inside the door. A graying mustache covered his upper lip, and a silver star dangled from his neck. He instructed Anderson to put everything from his pockets into a clear plastic bag. He then waved a whiny, metal detecting wand over Anderson and patted his hand quickly over his clothing. The marshal directed Anderson to walk ahead of him into the building.

I crossed my arms over my chest and called over the metal detector. "Don't you think you should put cuffs on him?"

Anderson furrowed his brow. "Come on, Jackie— Jack." He raised his hands for the marshal. "I'm no threat."

The marshal scowled as though resenting me telling him how to do his job and motioned Anderson forward again.

Luis tried to make nice, calling, "We'll be in touch soon, Mr. Anderson."

# CHAPTER 2

I picked Larry up from the motel the next morning. He tossed his bag into the back of my old, forest green Escort, and the wagon groaned onto the road. If this case paid the way Luis claimed, the first thing I planned to do is buy a new vehicle, something less conspicuous and more reliable.

The patchouli oil on Larry's tunic shirt would haunt the wagon for at least a week. I figured we could at least have breakfast before I dropped him off at the bus station. I didn't expect him to be angry when I handed him a check.

"You're leaving town!" Larry exclaimed. "I didn't come here for money, Jack. I helped you. Now I thought you were going to help me."

"I don't really have a choice."

Larry's brown mop-top hair waved as he shook his head back and forth. "You always have a choice."

"When one option is paying bills and the other leaves you homeless, it isn't much of a choice." I was exaggerating, of course. I could have said no— probably should have said no. "What kind of help do you need?"

"I told you I'm looking for a Native American priest or shaman familiar with shape shifter lore. There are reservations all around Albuquerque, and I thought you would help me find someone."

I felt myself getting angry at him again like I had the last time he had mentioned *shape shifters*. "I took you to the Indian Market. Besides, don't you think that's kind of culturally insensitive?"

"What do you mean?"

"The only Native Americans I know have real jobs. They aren't dancing around teepees and turning into animals." My mind drifted to Officer Allen Deschene, the policeman. I guessed he was probably Native American, although I had never thought much about it.

Larry's round glasses pointed at the road straight ahead. "Teepees are Plains Indians, Jack, not Pueblos. I'm being serious! You, of all people, know things like that exist."

My anger threatened to boil over. "What's that supposed to mean?"

"We've seen stuff, Jack. After what just happened with Alice on your last case, you can't tell me these legends and myths aren't based on reality!"

Sometimes I was certain Larry knew more about my missing years than I wanted to share, but then he would make me feel foolish for being angry. "You may have a point. Some myths could have a vague relationship to facts. I assumed this Native American thing was just another casual interest for you. I don't know anyone like that. You're the only person I know who I might call a spiritualist." I rolled the term *spiritualist* in my brain for a moment and decided it really did fit. "I'll brainstorm while I'm gone, see if I can think of anyone who can help."

"You'll forget all about it again."

Larry was into some weird stuff. It had come in handy on my last case, but it was hard to know what to take seriously and what was just some obscure interest or metaphysical belief he held. Evidently this was more important to him than I had realized.

"I won't forget," I said. "I promise. I'm going to make this trip as quick as I can. Believe me."

The Escort sputtered along a suburban street, and I pulled the car into a driveway of one of the ranch houses. As soon as I got out, I could smell burnt pancake batter and coffee. Albert Ellison answered the door wearing a green apron over an ochre dress shirt. His eyes regarded Larry, and the lips within his blond goatee spread into a smile. "Lawrence! I'm so glad you came!"

Alice was already sitting at the dining room table. She tried to stand when we entered. I grabbed her before she fell and helped her slide back into her seat. Her pale face flushed red with embarrassment. "Sorry," she said. "My muscles are still a little weak." Her sandy hair stubble was hidden beneath a musty, red stocking cap.

Her expression darkened when she noticed Larry. "Do I know you?"

"You might," Larry said.

"I think I dreamt about you once. You were… tying me up."

Albert poured juice into glasses and motioned for us to sit.

"Larry helped you," I said.

"Oh." She gave me a doubtful look before turning back to Larry who was now sitting across from her. "Then I guess I should say thank you."

We finished our breakfast quickly. Alice kept casting suspicious glances at Larry. My assurances could not erase whatever her subconscious remembered about their strange encounters. She insisted on standing again before we left and gave me an awkward hug. I thanked Albert for breakfast.

He took my hand in one of his and Larry's hand in the other. "No! I should be the one thanking you! You brought my daughter back to me. You are both welcome here any time!"

\* \* \*

Little Alpha pushed between my ankles into Diane's apartment and raced around Reece like a furry black cyclone while the boy giggled. At nine years old, Diane's son had sprouted past my waist, growing a full foot in less than a year. With his flawless cocoa skin and golden hazel eyes, he would break some hearts when he was older. He was a great kid, but I felt anxious around him. I worried something I said or did might somehow damage him, like a plant watered with herbicide. A toxic cloud hung over me, and I didn't want to see him smothered by it. I never wanted him to lose that childhood joy I saw in him when he played with the dogs.

I shook my head watching the old dog and the boy. "Alpha's no spring chicken, but look at him go. I don't know if he will ever outgrow his puppyhood."

Meega, however, trotted with deliberate steps to her spot behind the couch and lay down. Meega never showed as much energy as Alpha, but she usually had a burst of enthusiasm when she greeted Reece. Reece dangled his head over the back of the couch and scratched Meega behind her ear. "Aww. What's wrong, Meega?" The forty pound mutt thumped her tail a single time in response.

I frowned. "She's still sulking about getting locked in the pound, and now I'm leaving her again." I squatted so I could pat her furry rump, which was the only thing sticking out from behind the couch. "I wish I didn't have to go. I'll be back as soon as I can." I knew she didn't understand my words, but she must have sensed the emotion behind them. She turned and gave my hand a lick. Then her head sank back down and she closed her eyes.

I stood and shook my head. "I shouldn't be doing this."

Diane put a hand on my shoulder. "We'll take care of them. They like it here, and Reece loves having them around."

"I have no idea how long this could take. I've bound myself to Anderson again while the people I really care about are here. I feel like I've signed a contract with the devil."

"That's a little dramatic, don't you think?"

"No, I don't. Anderson's taken so much from me and now he's taking this as well."

"Well, if it gets to be too long, you can always fly back for the weekend and charge the flight against Anderson's retainer."

A grin spread across my face. "You always know just what to say."

# CHAPTER 3

I hated airports. So many people crowded past me, all of them surrounded by different smells. It was almost impossible to sort individual people from the mob. Someone could walk right up to me in the crowd and plug me in the back before I even knew they were there.

Even though I hadn't needed to draw my gun for two years, I still felt insecure without its weight. There was no way to carry it onto a plane. I could have packed it in my checked bag, but that seemed unnecessary, and Luis advised against it.

I watched my carry-on bag slide through the X-Ray machine and submitted to the TSA agent's brief pat down. "Shouldn't you at least buy me dinner first?" The agent didn't react to my joke. Perhaps it wasn't as original as I'd thought.

I'd asked Luis not to wear cologne if we were going to be stuck on a plane together, but I think he'd worn so much for so long that the scent permeated his pores. Travelling with Luis did have advantages, however. We were the first to board the plane, and I kicked my legs back and forth through the extra space in business class. When Luis ordered a drink, I followed his lead. I enjoyed thinking Anderson was paying the bill.

Once we were in the air, I retrieved my laptop from the overhead bin and scrolled through photos and files related to the case. Anderson's employer, Strateegis, had formed just as the Iraq war began in order to capitalize on a wealth of government contracts going to private security companies. They didn't have any current job listings on their website. After the wars in Iraq and Afghanistan started winding down, they'd likely cut back significantly on hiring.

Luis wrapped a neck pillow around his thick neck and closed his eyes. "You've been uncharacteristically quiet, Jack."

"What exactly are your intentions with Diane?"

"My intentions? What do you mean?"

"I know you went out on a date."

"A couple, actually. She's quite a woman. What are you, her dad?"

"She's your employee."

"More than just an employee. She practically runs the place. Your point?"

I was happy to hear him admit how crucial Diane was to his business. He was a glory hound and liked taking all the credit for everything, but Diane actually knew way more about the business side of things than Luis did.

"Exactly," I said. "What if things go south? If she leaves, she might take your business down with her. Besides, don't you usually go for blondes?"

"I guess I do have a type. Both my ex-wives were blonde." His chin wagged side to side. "One former cheerleader and one beauty pageant contestant. Maybe it's time to try something new." The corner of his mouth lifted in amusement, but I didn't try to hide my disgust. "I think you're exaggerating, Jack. It was just a couple of dinners. I know you don't get out much, but we aren't all dead. You can't tell me you haven't thought about it."

"Thought about what?"

"Come on, Jack. Diane watches your dog for you. You spend time with her kid."

"How did you—?"

"It doesn't take a PI to notice when she comes in late or leaves early to help you out. Are you jealous, Jack? Is that the problem?"

"Of course not! Just concerned. Diane is part of our family—our work family."

The unwanted image of Luis grunting on top of Diane flashed in my mind, and I thought I might throw up in my mouth. I'd never smelled either of them on the other, thankfully. I wasn't jealous. I just thought Diane deserved better, and it was risky business dating her boss. It could upset our work relationships and our friendship.

I scrolled through a list of items and photos on my computer screen. All the stolen items were originally in the same bin at the Iraq Museum. The crate contained cylinder seals, urns, a mask, coins.

"Where are the rings?" I asked.

"Jesus, Jack, I told you it was just a couple of dates."

"No, on the inventory. All of the stolen items were originally housed in the same compartment at the Iraq Museum before the invasion in 2003 when they went missing. The museum inventory lists five rings originally packed in the same lot, but there are no photos of rings with the items recovered in Anderson's storage unit. It looks like there is a bowl from that section still missing too."

I brought up screen shots from the Ebay page where Anderson had allegedly listed the items for sale. The Ebay listings had led the FBI right to Anderson's doorstep. The rings and bowl weren't listed there either.

Luis looked over my shoulder. "Rings are pretty small compared to the other items. The thief might have kept them as mementos, sold them separately, used them as bribes along the way. Maybe he gave them to his girlfriends."

"Or boyfriends. We don't want to make any assumptions." It would be easy to lose track of something that small. "The bowl is larger, seven inches high and fifteen inches in diameter, according to the museum description, but I suppose it could have gotten separated on the journey just as easily. Maybe someone is eating Lucky Charms out of it right now."

"That would hold a lot of cereal," Luis said.

I clicked another image, and a fractured stone relief showed a bearded man in profile. A scepter or something rested in one hand while he lifted the other hand skyward. The cracks in the stone were so severe that it reminded me of a jigsaw puzzle. Below the bearded figure, rows of men kneeled with bowed heads and upraised arms, but their hands were rounded and fingerless like a cartoon, even though the fingers on the man above were all well-defined. Adding to the cartoony feel, their faces were all in profile with torsos facing straight forward. A star above the scene cast beams of light down on them.

I continued clicking over documents. "It looks like the FBI has already collected all the evidence they need. I'm not really sure what our role is supposed to be."

"We look over what they already have," Luis said. "Find gaps, make connections they might have missed."

"And if they didn't miss anything?"

Luis gave me a broad grin. "Then we just made the easiest money of our lives."

# CHAPTER 4

Natural light from the skylights lit living greenery inside the Norfolk airport. I wanted to retrieve my bags and get outside as quickly as I could. I felt like the sooner I got to work, the sooner the job would be done. In reality, we might be waiting for the FBI and the prosecutors to do their thing before we could get anywhere near finished with this case. I carried the bags while Luis picked up our rental car.

Wisps of gray blew across an overcast sky. Any scrap of ground not covered in concrete was covered in green growing things. I could smell moisture in the air and wondered if it might rain. I'd forgotten the rest of the country wasn't as brown and dusty as Albuquerque. Virginia reminded me of spring back in Indiana, but somehow I had set up residence in a climate not unlike Afghanistan, where my youth had ended.

I hadn't paid much attention to the mermaid sculpture at the airport, but I noticed another on our drive downtown. She was identical in form but painted in wild, gaudy colors.

Luis led the way into a conference room with his hand extended to a blonde woman sitting at an elliptical table. Madeline Weinstein towered over Luis as she stood and shook his hand. She cast a suspicious look at me behind him. The faint odor of marijuana, too subtle for anyone else to detect, hung on her immaculate blue business suit.

She returned to her seat. "Let's get on with it." Weinstein's breath smelled of coffee, but she didn't offer us anything. "You already know I advised Anderson not to hire you."

My eyebrows lifted as Luis and I sat across from her. "You did?"

"I said as much on the conference call."

I'd been out of the room when Luis worked out the details.

Weinstein continued, "I advised Anderson to confess in exchange for a lighter sentence. When you see the evidence against him, you'll agree. There's no way out of this." She added, "Even though he did eventually turn himself in, running cost him. The court denied bail. Hiring someone with your reputation makes him look even more guilty."

My heart sank. The general public had forgotten all about me, but anyone working this case might discover my relationship to Anderson and my shame.

Weinstein placed a thick file folder between us on the table. I scooted it away from Luis and thumbed through it. "We've already got all this," I said.

She pulled out a sheet of paper with a list of about 100 names. "You haven't seen this. It's a list of the people the FBI is questioning on the case."

I scanned the page of meaningless names. I didn't even know where in the country, or outside the country, these potential witnesses might be located. We didn't have the resources of the FBI. How long would it take me to track them all down?

Weinstein must have seen the anxiety on my face. "Our best strategy, other than pleading guilty of course, would be to wait for the FBI's report and see who the prosecution thinks is worth deposing. Let them narrow down the list for us."

My voice was barely a whisper. "That could take forever."

"You might be surprised," Weinstein said. "The Eastern District of Virginia is the original Rocket Docket. I expect this entire case to be wrapped up in less than eleven months."

Eleven months was still almost a full year tied to Anderson.

Weinstein added, "Would have been much shorter if he'd taken my advice."

I shook my head and pushed the paper back at her. I wanted this case over and didn't want to wait. "Show the list to Anderson. See if he can narrow the names down for us. If there is someone on there who saw something, he should know."

"That's a great idea." Weinstein shoved the paper back at me. "I'll let you handle that. You are his friends and the *investigative consultants*."

I winced at the word *friends* and stared down at the paper. Talking to Anderson again on this case was inevitable, but I wasn't ready.

Luis grabbed the paper. "I'll ask him."

I nodded my thanks to him and then turned back to Weinstein. "I'd also like to see the stolen goods and where they were found."

Weinstein looked to Luis as if to ask if I was being serious. "The evidence is being held by the FBI. Their inventory and descriptions are very thorough, and one storage unit looks like any other."

Luis nodded. "You may be right, but Anderson is paying us a ridiculous sum of money. We might as well do something to earn it."

I was grateful and surprised to hear Luis back me up. I'd been thinking of him as a villain lately because of his relationship with Diane and how he had talked me into working this case, but he was treating this as my show. Despite how I had practically blackmailed Luis into mentoring me, I couldn't forget how much he'd done for me. I'd wandered into town two and a half years earlier with literally nothing to my name. He may not have taken me under his wing out of kindness, but, whatever the reason may have been, he'd gone above and beyond my expectations.

That being said, if I managed to survive this case, I think we would be more than even.

At least we didn't have to share a hotel room. The only noise in my room came from the fan in the air conditioner and a muffled television two rooms away. I thought about calling Diane, but she was probably busy. I settled for a text. Meega had slept the day away, but otherwise the dogs were fine. I considered going over my notes again, but there was nothing new to learn there.

I ordered ribs from room service and ate alone in the quiet. Instead of eating at the desk, I spread out on a bed one and half times the width of the one in my apartment and flipped through cable channels while I ate. I finally settled on a showing of the original *Wolfman* with Lon Chaney Jr., which I hadn't seen since I was a kid. I had never found it scary at all, even as a child, but I'd liked the monster's makeup and appreciated the foggy, forested soundstage.

Between commercials, a man in a funny wig and a lab coat made jokes and gave trivia about the movie.

*Even a man who is pure of heart and says his prayers by night, can become a wolf when the wolfbane blooms...* This is what the world pictured when they heard the word… I hesitated to even think the word… *werewolves.*

As a kid, of course, I hadn't realized how unrealistic the movie was. The film had invented much of its own mythology, which became better known than the old stories. I knew all too well that myths and folklore can be rooted in reality. I pushed the thought from my mind.

I had a lot of time to make up for. There was no point dwelling on the past and things I still didn't fully understand.

I had contemplated hitting the hotel pool before going to sleep but woke up an hour later with the television still on. I felt like there was something I needed to do, but there were no dogs here to walk, no animals to cradle. I turned off the television and the lamp and cocooned myself in blankets and pillows.

*** 

I hated this hallway. I despised this whole building, but especially this corridor. Even with the earplugs, "The Real Slim Shady" pounded in my years. When they had first started playing the song, I was so relieved to hear something new. I'd originally considered "Barbie Girl" a hilarious choice to play for a bunch of Islamic, Arab prisoners and chuckled about it with the other soldiers. After a few hundred times, the amusement shifted to annoyance.

At least I got to leave the building. The detainees were stuck with it night and day, nonstop. One of the prisoners had been driven so crazy that he had rammed his head against the cinderblock wall and was now restrained, face up. He couldn't even shield his eyes from the ever-present fluorescent lights long enough to sleep.

When they had finally started playing a new song, I hoped maybe they would at least play the whole freakin' album, but they looped the same track, over and over.

I had joined the Army to follow in my dad's footsteps. I expected to be shooting at bad guys and saving lives like a hero. Handing out toilet paper in this squalor didn't feel heroic.

One of the cells remained empty. We'd made a big show of removing the prisoner yesterday to be executed. In reality, he'd just been transferred to another corridor. We didn't have the authority to execute anyone, but some of us liked to act like we did.

I paused before the next cell and stopped breathing. An old man's wrists were threaded between his legs and cuffed to the wall behind him. Urine darkened the front of his orange jumpsuit, and his neck drooped, slack and still. His body hung in a crouch, unable to sit, but no longer able to stand. He'd been like that for over 24 hours at that point, and one of his shoulders looked dislocated. Sergeant Anderson had assured me he would order the man relieved, but here he still was.

I gingerly tapped on the bars. The man flinched, and I finally released my breath. He was still alive. I'd like to say I immediately grabbed the keys and unshackled him, but I turned away. As soon as I finished my task, I would bring my complaint to Anderson again and be more insistent. He'd have to listen this time.

I completed my task as quickly as possible to escape the sights and smells, but when I saw the line of prisoners shuffling in from the other direction, I slowed down. I didn't want my peers to know how much this job bothered me. I worried too much about what the other soldiers thought of me when I should have been worrying about other things.

Two guards prodded the five hooded men past me. The prisoners' naked skin glowed red from the pressurized water the soldiers had used to hose them clean. Zip-tied hands covered their genitals.

None of the guards wore nametags in the building because we didn't want to be identifiable, but I knew these two. O'Leary cocked his thumb back and pointed it at me like a gun, smirking the whole time. I returned the gesture and tossed a roll of toilet paper at him. I couldn't hear his muffled words clearly through the earplugs, but I accepted the cigarette he offered.

Donavan raised her camera and pointed at me, then to the prisoners. I smiled and repeated the cocking gun gesture O'Leary and I had exchanged, this time pointing at the naked men. The camera flashed. I didn't know it yet, but my life changed that moment and would never be the same.

I opened my eyes in the hotel bed, remembering. I'd had more nightmares in the last week than I remembered having over my entire life, even the years I had lived in the wild.

Donavan had finished out her term and left the service. She now owned a bakery in Colorado and was raising two kids with her husband. O'Leary had re-upped, got promoted to sergeant major and was serving stateside. I had become a criminal, a social pariah, disappeared from society for nine years and was only now finding some semblance of a normal, human life.

# CHAPTER 5

I woke up early and wasn't hungry for breakfast. We still had several hours before we were scheduled to meet with the lawyer again. I decided to get a head start on the day before Luis was up.

A chain link fence surrounded five simple, cinderblock buildings lined with wide, bright orange doors of corrugated metal. One gate to exit the fence could only be opened from the inside, and another gate to enter required a punch code. Cameras pointed at the gates. A moving van parked within the fencing, and three people moved boxes into one of the storage units. I tugged open the glass door of the connected office. No one sat behind the long counter, so I pushed a button, and almost immediately heard a male voice saying, "Be right there."

From somewhere in the back, a slender black man in a baseball cap emerged, followed by a thick cloud of cologne. "Are you interested in renting a unit?" he asked. The cologne was enough to make my eyes water but couldn't hide the scent of cigarette smoke.

I handed him a business card. "I'm working a case. My client, Thomas Anderson, is accused of stashing stolen antiquities in one of your units."

To my surprise, the man's mouth grew into an excited grin. "Yeah! The FBI was here all day a couple weeks ago. I had to call the head office. I'd never been served a warrant before!"

I couldn't help but smile at his reaction. He whipped out his phone and showed me photos of a black van with a white FBI logo stenciled on the side. Behind the cracked phone screen, men and women in FBI jackets carried stuff from one of the units, but none of the items they carried was clear enough to identify.

I asked, "Do you have camera footage of Mr. Anderson coming in and out of the building?"

He shook his head. "No, man. The FBI already asked. We only keep about two months of footage. I can get you a list of when his code was used to get in and out though, if you want."

"That would be great."

Cologne burned my nose while he tapped on a keyboard. I was eager to get out of that confined space with him. "Can I see the unit he used?"

He handed me the paper with a list of dates and times. "Not much to see, now. It's just an empty unit."

"Humor me."

He shrugged. "Sure. No one else has rented it yet."

"It's already available to rent to other customers?"

"Yup. FBI cleared it out."

I was happy to get outside where a breeze carried away some of the man's cologne. He unlocked a pedestrian gate beside the truck entrance. The man had long legs and a wide, side-to-side stride. After all the time on the plane and in the car, it was refreshing to walk at a brisk pace keeping up with him. He wound around the buildings straight to a particular unit. More useless cameras pointed at the intersections of the buildings. The units all looked alike to me, but he knew exactly which one it was and rattled up the big corrugated door. Within, as he had said, was nothing but a bare cement floor.

I detected the faint smell of dust and cardboard, but not even a speck of dirt marred the ground. "You were right. This place is spotless."

"The FBI even vacuumed the floor. Said the dust might be evidence. Can you believe that?"

I raised my eyebrows at him, then closed my eyes in the corner of the unit and took a deep breath through my nose. For a moment, I thought I got a whiff of fine sand and burning tree sap, but then I coughed on cologne. It stung the back of my throat.

"Thanks for humoring me," I said.

"No problem!"

I picked Luis up back at the hotel and chauffeured him to Weinstein's office.

A woman wearing a loose-fitting tan uniform strolled into the small conference room. Her dark hair wound into a tight braid behind her head, leaving only a few straggling black hairs on the back of her thick, muscular neck. She sat in the empty chair across the table from Weinstein, Luis and myself.

"Thank you for coming, Captain…" I hesitated over the last name.

"Just say, *nwhen*." She glared at me with dark eyes. "It's not like I had a choice, sir. I was ordered to talk to you."

"Captain Nguyen," I repeated, still not confident in the first consonant of her name. "You work in Logistics?"

She gave a terse nod. "Yes, sir."

The *sirs* took me right back to my Army days.

Luis interrupted. "I'm not familiar with the jargon. What exactly is *logistics?*"

Captain Nguyen shifted her gaze to Luis. "I managed the evening shift in the Army warehouse at Camp Victory. If a base in northern Iraq needed guns, I found another base with surplus and ordered them shipped. All United States property coming in or out of Iraq came through us."

"If that's the case," I said, "then the stolen artifacts must have gone through your warehouse at some point."

"Mr. Anderson was responsible for supplying his unit of civilian contractors. He spent a lot of time in the warehouse and had ample opportunity to sneak something into a conex going out. He had complete autonomy off base."

I nodded. "A conex is one of those large, metal shipping containers we see on the backs of trucks?"

Nguyen released a frustrated breath, as though this should be an obvious fact. "Yes, sir. We load them all onto a ship and from there they can be loaded one by one onto the back of a truck or a train."

Luis asked, "Did you check Anderson's crates before they went out?"

She furrowed her brow at Luis. "We checked most things going out, yes, but the contractors in his unit packed things tightly onto pallets and wrapped them in cellophane. We didn't cut open every single pallet and we didn't always see what was in the center."

"So…" I paused. "It almost sounds like you think Anderson is guilty."

"I have no doubt, sir."

"But, did you ever actually see him shipping artifacts out?" I asked.

"Well, no, sir," she said, "but he shipped things out all the time."

"But you don't know what."

She scrunched her nose as though smelling something foul. "It takes some balls for someone like you to question how I do my job."

My stomach tightened.

Weinstein intervened, "Mr. Mahler isn't the one being accused of a crime, Captain Nguyen."

"Not this time," she said under her breath.

I could feel my face getting red and I tightened my hand into a fist below the table. She'd obviously looked me up, but she never would have strayed from the dutiful *sirs* if we weren't civilians. We all stared at her, waiting.

"No," she said "I don't know what he was shipping out. No one does. That in itself makes him look guilty. You know he ran a gambling ring? It wasn't enough for him to make three times what I did for the same job. He was making money off the servicemen too. "

"It wouldn't surprise me," I said.

Luis jabbed my thigh under the table with his pen. "Did a lot of people owe him money?"

She shrugged a shoulder. "A few."

"Did you owe him money?" I asked.

She inhaled through her nose. "I paid all my debts." After a long silence, Captain Nguyen finally said, "Are we done here?"

We looked to each other and Weinstein said, "Thank you for your time, Captain."

Captain Nguyen scooted the chair loudly away from the table and pushed out the door.

Weinstein folded her arms. "You see? This was pointless. Anderson thought that woman would be a witness for the defense! Her testimony would only make him look more guilty."

"We already knew Anderson was sleazy," I said. "Her testimony doesn't add anything to the prosecution's case either. She didn't actually see anything."

Weinstein stood. "Do you think that will matter to a jury? We can't let this go to trial!"

I silently agreed with Weinstein, but this was Anderson's money, and if he wanted to waste it, that wasn't my fault.

# CHAPTER 6

The smooth paved road seemed out of place surrounded by acres of swamp. I cracked open a window and inhaled strange pollens mixed with mud. Luis pulled the car up to an empty gatehouse in the middle of the abandoned road. He pushed a button and announced who we were. The mechanical arm lifted and we continued driving past a large obstacle course with climbing ropes and zip lines. Grass almost grew over a line of curved barbed wire meant for trainees to crawl under. Closer to the main building was a mockup of a city street with burned out buildings and broken windows.

"Zachary King is a big fish," Luis said. "Let me do the talking."

I continued staring out the window.

"Are you listening to me, Jack?"

"Gotcha. Don't talk to the king fish."

"Get all the smart-ass out now. Once we get in there, I don't want to hear a peep. We're lucky this guy agreed to talk to us at all."

"As long as it's just us. He specifically said *no lawyers*. Kind of odd."

"Lots of people hate lawyers, Jack."

"Lots of people hate private investigators too, but he's talking to us."

We parked at a two-story building of beige brick. Only two other cars were parked in the lot. The BMW faded into the background behind the flashy, red Ferrari. The building was eerily silent, but we followed a sign and finally found a secretary typing at his computer. He picked up a phone and directed us into an open office door.

King sat at a large desk in front of a window overlooking the obstacle course. A couch lay off to the side of the room, and another door on the opposite wall led to more rooms. A bookshelf held new books on military strategy as well as classics by Sun Tzu and Machiavelli.

I can't quite explain why I had such an immediate negative impression of King. He was about ten years older than me, but appeared to be in much better shape. His white, button-down shirt hugged firm muscles, and he carried himself with a relaxed confidence, even while sitting down. He smelled of fresh soap and his breaths came easy and deep. He'd probably just showered after a mid-afternoon workout. Zachary King had single-handedly founded this company and grown it from nothing.

"Come in, gentleman. I'm sorry I had to put off meeting with you. I've been in D.C. most of the week. My secretary says you want to talk about Thomas Anderson, but you're not with the FBI."

"No," Luis handed him a business card, but King didn't take it.

"Oh, I know who you are." He cast a sideways glance at me that made me nervous. "My lawyers told me not to talk to you, but I've got nothing to hide. Water?" He pulled two plastic bottles from the mini-fridge behind him and handed them over the table.

I waved them away, but Luis leaned forward in his chair and took an offered bottle. He sat up straight, imitating King's posture. Luis even altered his speaking style slightly to be more like King. "Thank you, Mr. King. I assure you, this is just an informal meeting. We only want to touch base with you about our client's case."

King sat back in his chair, and Luis relaxed his posture. Luis and King held their hands on the plastic lids as though not wanting to be the first to open their waters. King finally cracked, and Luis twisted open his bottle as well. King brought the bottle to his lips like he was about to drink but brought it back down at the last moment. Luis, attempting to mirror the action, spilled some of the water on his shirt.

King laughed and handed over a paper towel. Mirroring is an old technique alleged to build a rapport by making yourself seem familiar to the person you are questioning. You attempt to subtly mimic a person's mannerisms and that supposedly makes them more comfortable with you. When it works, the person you are mirroring will start mirroring you without realizing it. It didn't work as well on someone like King, who had probably used the same technique and must have spotted what Luis was doing. It didn't help that Luis was not as subtle or as smooth as he liked to think.

I don't know about making him comfortable, but in this case, it certainly gave King a good laugh. On another occasion, I might have found it amusing as well, but I settled back in the chair without a word like a dutiful sidekick.

With their game over, King took a large gulp of water. "My lawyers said if I did speak with you, they wanted to be here. I told them to go to hell."

"I appreciate your trust, Mr. King." Luis blotted his shirt. "In other instances where your employees got into trouble, you paid to defend them in court. Did you or your lawyers offer to help Anderson?"

King shook his head. "If Anderson took those artifacts, he deserves to be put in jail."

Consistent with old habits, I spoke before I thought. "What if we think you took them?"

I caught a not-so-subtle wince from Luis. He didn't want me to talk at all, and when I spoke, I pushed way too hard.

To my surprise, King laughed again. "You can't possibly believe that, but I understand you have to throw it out there. With a client as guilty as yours looks, you've got to grasp for any straws you can. If you're lucky, maybe one of those straws will say something just stupid enough to cast suspicion on them and present a possible scenario where your client didn't steal those artifacts. That's why my lawyers didn't want me to see you, to protect me from any word games you might play, but I've got nothing to fear. Anderson did all of our on-site shipping and all the artifacts were found in his storage unit. There is nothing to tie me or anyone else at my company to the artifacts. Hell, any money we might get from stolen antiquities would dwarf what the government was paying us legally."

I was on a roll. "It looks like a ghost town around here. How long has it been since you had one of those juicy government contracts?"

King narrowed his eyes, but he never stopped smiling and his relaxed posture never changed. "Administrations change. The contracts are smaller, but we still do work for the United States government and others. It's only a matter of time before the country needs us again. Why would I put that at risk just to stuff some ancient trash in someone else's storage unit? The only thing I'm guilty of is not screening my employees well enough."

My mouth tightened. "That's one thing we agree on."

Luis didn't disguise his anger with me that time. "I think that's enough, Jack."

"You're one to talk," King said. "I've never hired anyone who was kicked out of the service. I was curious when I found out Anderson had hired you. I wanted to see what kind of person the infamous Specialist Jack Mahler really was. If the government had put Strateegis in charge of that detention center, you never would have been allowed near those prisoners."

My face flushed red from both anger and embarrassment. After so many years, most people had forgotten all about the scandal. King wasn't most people. He thought he knew all about me. I could have done more to stop the abuse eleven years ago, but the man in charge and the man who should have been kicked out of the service was the man King had hired and the man who had most likely stolen those artifacts while working for him.

The lawyer, Nguyen, King— was there anyone on this case who didn't know about my disgrace? I felt naked in the chair, but instead of being shamed, it made me angry.

My fist clenched as I tried to make the rest of my body appear relaxed. "Anderson isn't the first Strateegis employee to be involved in a scandal. You really think your mercenaries could do a better job than the U.S. Army?"

Luis placed a firm hand on my leg before I could say anything more. "I'm sorry for my colleague. Maybe *I* should also be screening *my* employees better." Luis glared at me and paused, daring me to speak again. Then he turned back to King. "We aren't here to accuse anyone. We're just collecting information and we want to know if you or anyone in your company saw anything that could be helpful. It's someone else's job to decide guilt or innocence."

"Well said, Mr. Navarro." King challenged me again with his eyes before continuing. "After the news broke, I personally led an extensive investigation of all my people who worked with Anderson at that time. It's been a few years, but I keep good records and maintain good relationships with my former employees—except for people like Anderson, of course. I've already provided all this to the FBI. I can send a copy of my report to Ms. Weinstein if she likes."

Luis nodded. "That would be very helpful."

"If that's all you need, I have a lot of work I need to finish up before the end of the day." King aimed one more challenging glance at me.

Luis stood. "Thank you again for meeting with us."

We left the secretary behind us, and I whispered, "I wonder who else King hires himself out to?"

Luis spoke through clenched teeth. "It's been a long time since we worked a case together, Jack. An investigator is supposed to be discreet. You get more information using honey than you do with vinegar."

It felt good to get out of the stuffy building and into the parking lot surrounded by fields and trees. "Discreet? Is that what those TV commercials you do are supposed to be?"

Luis stopped walking and looked me in the eye. "You are in rare form today. Have you forgotten that we are supposed to be a team? If I didn't know better, I'd think you were deliberately trying to sabotage this case! I know you don't want to be here, but you agreed to take this case, and I expect you to do your job. You've grown into a damn good detective in the last two years. Don't screw that all up now! I know this brings up a lot of bad memories for you, but you can do this. Get your head in the game!"

I was ready for a shouting match, ready to be all angry and self-righteous, but Luis had actually mixed a compliment into his lecture. It completely disarmed me. "I think the reason I've been able to do well in the past is because I'm detached from the people I'm investigating. It's just a job. I don't care who is guilty and who is innocent. I don't have a personal stake. This is different."

Luis almost laughed. "That's bullshit, Jack."

"What?"

"You are always becoming too involved. When I first started training you, I warned you about getting emotionally caught up in your cases. It can bias you and cause you to miss important details. But, look at Alice McGuiness. Was she just a job? I'd have filled out the paperwork on that case and let it go. You kept digging. Getting personally involved can be messy. Half the time, your obsessive persistence annoys the hell out of me, but that time it paid off— for both of us. You like to act tough and say you don't care, but that's not the way a person who doesn't care acts, and everyone can see it, Jack. It's your greatest weakness, but it can also be your greatest strength. If I were in trouble, I'd want you fighting for me, and I'd trust you to do what was right, no matter how you felt about me."

I crossed my arms in the car and watched the trees roll by. He was right, and I hated him for it. Luis was self-absorbed and seemed oblivious to people's feelings, but understanding people was one of the skills Luis had used to build his business. "I suppose you might have a point."

"What was that?" Luis asked. "Was that Jack Mahler agreeing with me? This case must have you more messed up than I thought!"

"Very funny."

# CHAPTER 7

We parked in a visitor lot in front of a wide, three-story building of white concrete and gleaming glass. The only way for visitors to drive past the black iron gate in front of the building was by stopping at a transparent guardhouse. The smell of wet earth and fertilizer hovered over the grounds. Green grass had only now started to fill in the lawn around the new construction. Other businesses sat at the other side of the business park, across a retention pond. I still marveled at how much water was here compared to Albuquerque.

In the bowels of the building, a man in a black suit adjusted his glasses as he peered into a computer monitor. He sat behind a long, narrow desk, and behind him was a steel door. Two round globes in the corners above him housed wide angle cameras which could see the entire corridor behind me and probably what the man was typing on the screen as well.

"May I help you?" he asked.

Before I could respond, Luis placed his card on the desk. "I'm Luis Navarro, and this is my associate, Jack Mahler. Madeline Weinstein called ahead. We're here to look at evidence in the Thomas Anderson case."

The agent glanced at the card and peered at us over his glasses. "You'll have to wait for the agent in charge. In the meantime, I'll need to see your IDs."

The guard in front of the building had already made copies of all our identification, but I handed over my passport and PI license without complaint. The agent didn't seem to have any problem with the out-of-state PI licenses. I looked at the walls around me, but there was nowhere to sit as he scanned my identification into his computer.

The door clicked open behind him, and a man and woman in black suits exited. I caught a glimpse of metal wire walls and rows of metal shelving before the door swung shut again. The woman signed a clipboard and left.

The black man remained. Rounded cheeks softened his jaw line, and white peppered the short, black hair on his temples. "You must be Jack Mahler and Luis Navarro."

I thought I saw Luis' lips tighten a little when the agent said my name first instead of his.

The agent handed business cards to both of us. "I'm William Wittman, the agent in charge of the Anderson case."

If I squinted, Agent Wittman could look like one of the pixilated FBI men who had entered the storage unit. I nodded, and we signed a logbook. They made me stash my laptop bag behind the desk. I guess they didn't want me tossing any evidence into it and sneaking it away. Wittman and the man in glasses each waved a badge over one of the two sensor plates on either side of the door, and it clicked open. Agent Wittman then used a metal key to unlock a wire door, revealing a giant room of wall-to-wall shelving which seemed to fill the entire level.

I'd never been in an FBI evidence room before. I thought about snapping a picture with my phone, but I didn't want to look like a tourist. The room smelled of floor wax with a hint of lubricating oil on the moveable shelving. Musty paper hid inside bags and boxes. From somewhere deep in the room, I caught a whiff of dried blood.

"I assume you are mostly interested in seeing the artifacts," Wittman said.

"Of course," I said. "What else is there?"

"We confiscated a rifle and two pistols. Firearms are tagged and stored in a separate cabinet."

# BURIED CURSES

Agent Wittman escorted us around the musty shelves and unlocked a cage at the side of the room. A white couch leaned vertically against one of the wire walls.

"You took his couch?" I said.

"We confiscated everything in the storage unit. Anything that isn't stolen or illegal will be returned after the case is done."

Wittman removed a tarp from a crate, revealing individual items in labeled bags and boxes. Even the crinkly plastic shrink wrap that had been used to bind the items on its pallet was now folded into a tagged, transparent plastic bag. I reached down, but before I had gotten anywhere near the crate, agent Wittman handed me white gloves. I circled the crate, afraid I'd damage the ancient items just by touching them, even through the plastic bags and the gloves.

For all the anticipation though, the objects themselves were anticlimactic. I had no idea what most of these monochromatic beige items were supposed to be. The first item I focused on was a modern, mangled combination disc lock with the narrow metal shackle completely separated from the body. The FBI hadn't been gentle breaking into the unit.

Luis, now wearing ill-fitting gloves, picked up a bag containing a sculpture of a man carrying what might be a lion over his shoulders. With the material so eroded, the detail was impossible to make out. "Think how much all this would be worth!"

Wittman shook his head. "These items are too hot to be worth anything. No one would risk buying them. The Iraqi government is eager to get them back, and we're eager to see them gone. The sooner this case is closed, the better."

Mixed in with the artifacts were anachronistic items from Anderson's own past. I lifted a bag containing a wooden cassette case. A printed label on the bag listed the name of each cassette. "Talk about artifacts!" I didn't need to look at the label or open the bag to see the flashy band names printed on the edge of the plastic cases: bands like Kiss, Poison, even an old, guitar heavy Devil Yell cassette.

I pulled out a box with about a dozen ancient coins. Inside another bag, I discovered rings. "These must be the rings we talked about, Luis! They weren't listed on the Ebay listing or the FBI inventory."

When opened, the bag emitted a cloud of charred wood and roses, a scent I hadn't expected from old artifacts. Tightly wound gold wire formed one of the rings. A flat black disc adorned a ring with lines and curves etched on its face. Another was a simple copper band.

Wittman produced some papers from a folder and showed the last page, which clearly listed *four rings*.

I took the papers and frowned. "Our copy must have cut off the last page. The museum manifest listed five." It would indeed be easy to lose track of one small ring. I wondered what would happen if I slipped one of the ugly little things into my pocket. Agent Wittman wasn't watching me that closely, but there were cameras everywhere. I began thumbing through Wittman's list, scanning for the missing bowl when a deep voice interrupted from behind me.

"A good eye." The thin, angular man stood with his back to the cage wall. His white, button-down shirt and tan slacks did not match the dark-suited agents I had seen in the building so far.

I hadn't known anyone else was in here with us, and the brown-skinned stranger had startled me. The crate wasn't tall enough to hide anyone unless perhaps they were crouching. I was a hard person to sneak up on, especially in this quiet, echoey room. Perhaps he had been leaning in the shadow of the couch.

The dark man's eyes grew, and his mouth hung open when he saw me. "Enkidu?"

"What was that?" I asked.

"The rings?" Wittman asked.

"No, Ann…" I struggled to repeat what the stranger had said "…kidu?"

The stranger's face returned to a mask of calm, and he bowed his head to me. "My apologies." He annunciated with emphasis, as though English wasn't his native language, but he didn't have a foreign accent. "I thought I recognized you. You likely have not heard my name. Have you heard the name *Jules Castor?*"

I nodded, recognizing the name from the reports. "The man who authenticated these items for the FBI."

Wittman pulled another paper from his folder. "The artifacts were authenticated by an appraiser named Jules Castor."

I gave the agent a confused look, wondering why he felt the need to repeat the introduction.

Castor unwrapped a small, engraved cylinder and rolled it over his ungloved palm. Wittman didn't object, so I guessed authenticators must be allowed to do things like that. "These are cylinder seals. You rolled it over clay or wax to replicate the image on the cylinder. This image was someone's identity, more precious than a person's signature in your world of today." He picked up a curved clay fragment, still not using gloves. "If anyone tampered with your mail in ancient Mesopotamia, you would immediately notice the envelope had been broken."

I hate to admit it, but I was getting bored. None of these items seemed as exciting as I had imagined they would be. I just wanted to get this case over. "If the envelopes were made of clay," I said, "how did the mailman keep from breaking them all?"

Castor didn't respond. Instead Luis called from the cage entrance. "Breaking them?"

"These envelope fragments," I said.

Castor lifted a large, plastic bag containing a life-sized, bronze face. Metal coiled into simulated braids hanging from its sculpted chin. The authenticator gazed sadly at the hole where its eye had once been. "King *Sarrukin*, the first to unite all Mesopotamia. Humanity may have begun in Africa, but civilization began in Iraq. Do you think humans did that by themselves?"

I hope he didn't notice me rolling my eyes. "I'm sure Yahweh, Jesus, or Allah helped."

"Helped stop the mailman from breaking envelopes?" Luis asked. It was uncharacteristic for Luis to make a joke around the FBI agent. Giving authority figures a hard time was more my shtick. He and Agent Wittman were now whispering just beyond the door to the cage.

Castor chuckled softly. "Yahweh became a minor god in the Canaanite pantheon a few hundred years after these items were created. Those other names would be meaningless for another 2,000 years."

That did inspire a little awe. The three major religions of the planet seemed to me like they had been around forever. I had never imagined a time when they didn't exist. These knick-knacks of worn clay and bronze were older than anything familiar to me. "You're the expert," I said, trying to sound unimpressed.

"I wouldn't say that," Wittman said. "I'm pretty confused at the moment."

I couldn't believe agent Wittman would insult his authenticator like that, but Castor seemed to agree, shaking his head vigorously. "Castor knows nothing. Your historians know how old the antiquities are and a general idea of what region they came from, but to really understand the significance of an item, you need to speak the language."

He pointed at the bag of rings still in my hand, and I suddenly noticed an inscription on the inside of one of the rings. I activated the light on my phone to get a better look, but the cuneiform scratches weren't like any letters I had ever seen.

"That is the name of a low-ranking god. No one alive today can pronounce the name. There is power in language and pronunciation. To understand a word's power, you must be able to speak it."

I still stared at the scratchy symbol in the light from my phone. "I doubt anyone has spoken these languages in thousands of years."

"I'm sure you are right," Wittman agreed.

"Are you talking to yourself, Jack?" Luis asked.

This was an odd question. The crate wasn't tall enough to hide Castor standing right next to me.

"You don't see…" When I looked back, Castor was gone. I circled all the way around the crate. His back had been to the cage wall. There was no visible way out without shoving past one of us. "Where did he go?"

"We are the only ones who entered this room," Agent Wittman said.

"I just had a conversation with him! Jules Castor! You said it yourself. He authenticated these items for you."

A tiny blood vessel pulsed at the side of Agent Wittman's forehead. "I know who Jules Castor is. He isn't even in the country right now, Mr. Mahler."

Luis shook his head at me, a silent attempt to stop me, but I pressed on. "I wasn't talking to myself just now!" I had seen things that weren't really there before, but I thought that was all behind me. If I couldn't trust my own perceptions, what good was I as an investigator?

Agent Wittman locked the cage and escorted us out of the room. We reviewed the door entry logs and camera footage. We were the only three visible people in the cage. While Agent Wittman and Luis talked by the doorway, I appeared to be talking to myself. I tried to pinpoint when Castor had picked up the big bronze head, but nothing in the crate appeared to move.

Wittman folded his arms. "Your reputation precedes you, Mr. Mahler. We are not people you want to be playing with."

I looked at the camera image again, scanned the same scene from a different angle and got a view from the other side of the leaning couch. I didn't see any place Castor could have been hiding. "I really thought there was someone there."

Wittman cast a glance at Luis. "Your record is far from spotless, Mr. Mahler. Perhaps it is time we look at you with more scrutiny."

That sent a chill through me. I had a background check on file. They'd undoubtedly looked at it before they let me in here. They obviously already knew I'd been kicked out of the military eleven years ago. Between that time and two years ago, I had no records. It was as though I had ceased to exist for nine years. I suppose in a way I had. What could they possibly find?

Luis remained silent until we got to the car. "I know you do things your own way, Jack, and I know you didn't want this case, but this is ridiculous!"

"I really saw someone!" I hesitated. "At least I thought I did." After my last nightmarish case, how could I trust my own eyes?

A dark crimson sprang over Luis' face. "You didn't just embarrass yourself back there! If you and Anderson weren't friends—"

"We are not friends!"

"If he didn't specifically hire you, I'd pull you off this case and never work with you again!" He started the engine and squealed out of our parking spot. I'd seen Luis annoyed plenty of times, but I'd never seen him lose his cool like that before. By the time we reached the gate to the lot, he was calm enough to smile at the guard.

I wanted to apologize, but bringing it up would just piss him off again, and I wasn't sure which part I should be sorry for. I was sorry that I had seen something he didn't, but that wasn't my fault. I should have played it off like I really was talking to myself and saved face. If Castor had been a figment of my imagination, then I really had been talking to myself, so perhaps it wouldn't have been a lie.

Maybe I needed to see a psychiatrist and get on some medication. With all the genuinely strange things I'd seen, it felt impossible to know what was real and what wasn't. If my perception was compromised, how could I continue working this case? How could I be an investigator at all? It had taken me two years to build myself into a legitimate PI. What other job could I do if I didn't have this?

# CHAPTER 8

When we got back to the hotel, Luis invited me to eat dinner with him. It was a nice gesture after a frustrating day, but I wasn't hungry. When I got back to my room, I whipped out my laptop.

I couldn't find any references to *Sarrukin* or *Ann-kidu*, but I wasn't sure of my spelling. I googled *Jules Castor*. The bald, dark-bearded man on my screen was not the same person I had spoken to in the property room. Castor worked at a local auction house. He was currently scheduled to speak at a conference in France on how dealers and auction houses can help track down stolen antiquities.

A light rapping knocked on my door. The only person I thought it could be was Luis. Without even checking the peep hole, I flung the door wide and looked out upon an empty hallway. I stuck my head out and looked from left to right, not seeing a single person. Perhaps it was a kid playing a prank.

I shut the door, returned to the little desk and gazed at the appraiser's image on my screen. After a deep breath, I phoned Jules Castor and left a voicemail, trying to control the shakiness in my voice as I identified myself. I wasn't sure what I would have said if he had answered, but I didn't know what else to do.

Another knock tapped on the door. This time, I peeked out the peep hole instead of opening it. Again I saw nothing but an empty hallway. I continued looking out, waiting for another knock. Finally I turned away, and then the door knocked again.

I jerked the door open and stepped into the hallway with my chest puffed out, ready to confront someone. I wasn't in the mood to be messed with. No one was there. If it were a kid, they were probably nearby, chuckling around a corner or inside a neighboring room, but I didn't hear anything. I closed my eyes and inhaled a subtle scent of burning amber and rosewater.

I jumped when the phone trilled and lifted it up to my face. "This is Jack."

A deep, sleepy voice with a mild French accent responded. "This is Jules Castor. Did you just call me? Something about the stolen Iraqi artifacts?"

I turned back to the inside of my room. "Yes. Thank you for getting back with me so quickly."

"Do you know what time it is in France right now?"

I shut the door and paced as I spoke. "No. No, I'm sorry." The six-hour time difference hadn't even occurred to me.

"What are your questions?"

Now I felt on the spot. I was grasping at straws calling him out of the blue, and he was already annoyed. "Do you know how to pronounce the inscriptions on the artifacts?"

"Well, not exactly. Those languages haven't been spoken for thousands of years."

"Not since the time of King Sarrukin?"

That actually provoked a small chuckle. "You have indeed been doing your research, haven't you? Sarrukin is believed to be a more accurate pronunciation of the name Sargon, although some believe the *S* was pronounced more like an *L*..."

I tried not to sound too bored. "So there is no one alive today who can read the inscriptions as they were originally heard?"

Castor paused for a moment. "Well… no. I am surprised this would interest you. It has no bearing on the case, but I applaud you for taking an interest. Hold on…"

In the background, I heard a keyboard clicking.

"Take this down…" He read off the name *Aarif Bulsara* and a phone number. "He is the world's foremost glottochronologist—

claims he can trace changes in pronunciation backward in time. Maybe he can give you some ideas."

"Thank you."

"Now, if there is nothing more, I'm giving a presentation first thing in the morning."

"Have you heard of a person named *Annkidu?*"

"Ann-kidu...? I don't believe so. Wait, are you saying *Enkidu*, from the Epic of Gilgamesh?"

"Maybe."

He chuckled again. "You must tell me where you are finding your sources!"

"Just, uh, Google."

"That is a very odd pronunciation. I thought you were talking about someone alive today, a linguist perhaps."

"Can you tell me who this... Enkidu was?"

"You must know if you found such a rare pronunciation of the name. Enkidu, the wild man, companion to hero Gilgamesh."

"Uh-huh."

"You are an interesting person, Mr. Mahler. Don't hesitate to call if you have more questions. "

"Thank you. Sleep well."

I exhaled loud and long, trying to decide if any of that was helpful. Then I checked the clock and dialed Aarif Bulsara's university office number. I left a voicemail and then typed his name into my browser.

A photo came up and my breath caught in my throat. It was the man I'd seen in the property room! This must mean something. I considered calling Agent Wittman, but what good would that do? There was still no camera footage of him in the property room, no matter what his name turned out to be. I remembered the odd way he had introduced himself. He had never actually said his name was Jules Castor. He had said the name, and I assumed the rest. I'd explained away the odd phrasing because I assumed English wasn't his native language. I dialed Bulsara's home number, but the voicemail was full.

I still didn't initially get any hits on Enkidu until I found a link to Gilgamesh and corrected my spelling. Gilgamesh was one of the oldest heroes in literature, from thousands of years before Hercules, Achilles or Noah. He was aided by his best friend and sidekick, Enkidu, a wild man of the forest.

Castor, Bulsara, or whoever he was, had called *me* Enkidu! But I was no wild man of the woods, at least, not anymore. My stomach tightened. I was not an animal. There was no way he could have known my secret. I was just a man now, like any other.

# CHAPTER 9

My conscious mind whispered when the sheets shifted. Alpha must have jumped down and was now hopping back onto the bed. A faint smell of coppery blood danced across my nostrils, and I wondered what the little dog had been rolling in. He normally circled once, cuddled up against my leg and fell asleep, but he scooted over the blanket to the head of the bed. He gripped my shoulder and shook it as though he were a person trying to shake me awake.

My eyes drifted open and I noticed the hallway light through the tiny peephole in the hotel room door. This wasn't my apartment, and Alpha was back in Albuquerque! I sat up and fingers tightened on my shoulder, but I didn't see anyone in the room with me. I batted at my shoulder and reached for the gun beside my bed, but that was back in Albuquerque too. I tore the blanket from me and whatever had gripped me came off with it.

I flipped on the lamp and watched the blanket ripple. The thing was smaller than Alpha, but way too big to be a bed bug. It grabbed my leg from under the blanket. I jerked the fabric, but the blanket remained hooked on where the thing gripped me. I kicked it loose and ripped the blanket from the bed.

My feeling of being grabbed was all too accurate. Fingers pulled a human hand forward like a spider with five legs. It dragged a short, ragged stump and splintered radius bone across the white hotel sheets. Black hairs curled over its tan knuckles, wrist and the fragment of forearm that weighed it down. Somehow, the little hairs made the thing creepier, less like something out of a Hollywood movie and more real.

I half leapt and half fell from the bed. Its fingers flexed, launching it into the air. I caught it by the severed wrist just as it was about to hit my face. The smashed radius protruded an inch longer than the broken ulna. The bones rotated clockwise like a cyclone, and the fingers spread wide. The hand slipped from my grasp and landed knuckles first onto carpet. It flipped itself over and crawled into the shadows under the bed.

I stood still and quiet, listening, trying to think of some rational explanation. This was no nightmare. I breathed deeply, fully awake now, and the lamp lit the area around the bed clearly. I slowly reached for my phone on the charger, and still no sound came from under the bed. The only thing I could hear in the room was my own breathing. I flipped on the phone's light and crouched down.

The hand scurried out at me with impossible speed propelled by its five digits. I dropped the phone and tumbled backward, hitting the back of my head on the end table as I batted the thing away. My own hand found the little trashcan under the desk and flipped it upside down over the appendage.

It punched the inside of the plastic can, causing it to jostle forward. I sat on it, panting while the plastic thumped.

This was no illusion. Most people wouldn't be able to detect it, but I could smell the coagulated blood from the ragged stump and splintered bone. Now that I had it trapped, what could I do with it? For a small hand, it was pounding hard against its plastic prison. I scanned the room for something heavy to place on top of the trashcan. My travel bag might be heavy enough to keep one tiny hand down, but it was too large to balance on top of the trashcan, and pulling it over would leave me holding the can with only one arm.

The bumps came slower, speeding up at irregular intervals, but then slowing even more. The little thing seemed to be tiring itself out. The heavy blanket lay on the floor nearby from when I had thrown it off the bed. I wrapped it around the base of the can and waited for the thing to stop moving. I took a deep breath, tore off the can, and covered it with the blanket. I felt through the fabric as I bundled it into a ball, but I couldn't feel anything inside. I tried to keep the blanket folded together as I flattened it on the floor. Clearly nothing hid within the folds. I shook it flat, just to be sure. Had it escaped, or had it never been there in the first place?

I still smelled the blood, but now it was tinged with the scent of roses and charcoal. I flipped on all the lights and circled the room, sniffing and listening as I went. There weren't that many places it could hide in the small room, but a hand didn't need much space to hide in. The light on my phone had automatically switched off. I flipped it on again and scanned under the dresser and tables. I opened the closets while sniffing the air, but the smell led me back to the bed and empty blanket.

A faint strip of brown streaked the white sheets where the hand had crawled over the bed. The blood wasn't liquid. It had coagulated and dried into a moist, flakey powder. I probably could wipe it clean with a damp paper towel. The hotel maid service wouldn't even bat an eye.

The clock read 4:50 am. There was no way I could sleep in that room anymore tonight. I headed downstairs to use the exercise room before breakfast started at 6:00.

I ate breakfast in my workout clothes. I hadn't eaten dinner and shoveled scrambled eggs into my mouth. I'd heard stories about low blood sugar affecting perception. Perhaps I'd had a waking dream. After the strange encounter in the evidence room, my brain was already primed for weirdness.

Perhaps the man in the evidence room wasn't real either. Perhaps I was having a psychotic break. How could I know those nine years in the desert hadn't all been one long mental breakdown? It made more sense than what I believed had happened. The last two years had been a brief return to sanity, but now I was having a relapse.

I started laughing at the ridiculousness of it all. A couple of people in the breakfast room looked at me strangely, but most ignored me, continuing to eat.

After eating, I couldn't put off returning to my room any longer. I slowly pushed open the door, listening for movement within. Sunlight streamed into the big window onto the blanket on the floor and the trashcan on its side. I had to strain my eyes to see the narrow brown trail on the white bed sheet. I placed warm water on a Kleenex and the faint streak wiped away as though it had never been there.

After a warm shower and change of clothes, I again scanned the room, listening for movement, but the sunlit room was like another world compared to the nightmare reality of the early morning.

I called Larry. He didn't answer, and I didn't leave a voicemail. We hadn't parted on the best of terms. He had accused me of not being there for him and here I was calling just because I needed his advice about ghosts and spirits again. If none of this was real, he just might feed my delusion anyway. But he had helped me solve a case, hadn't he? Everyone acted as though we had solved a case. That couldn't have all been a delusion.

I shoved all my things into my bags and carried them to the front desk. I introduced myself, "Jack Mahler, room 319. Would it be possible to change my room?" I asked.

The man at the counter seemed surprised. "Is there something wrong?"

"I… saw a bug."

He tapped on a keyboard and looked at a screen. "Oh! We take that very seriously. Where did you see it?"

The best lies contain an element of truth. "In the bed."

I thought I saw the desk clerk looking around to see if anyone else had heard me, but I couldn't trust my own senses. "What did it look like?"

"It was big. I kicked it off the sheets and it ran under the bed."

The man seemed relieved it wasn't a bed bug. "I'm sorry that happened to you, sir. We can move you this afternoon."

"Great. In the meantime, can I stash my bags down here?"

A man in a business suit was now waiting in line behind me.

"Certainly, sir. I'm sorry for any inconvenience." The clerk attached tags to the bags and put them in a storage room.

"One more thing," I said. "Has anyone ever reported seeing anything strange here?"

"I assure you, our cleaning staff inspects every room before—"

"No, I mean... I heard some of the hotels in the area are haunted."

The clerk exchanged a glance with the man in line behind me. "I've never heard anything like that, sir."

I shrugged. "I didn't think so. Thanks."

# CHAPTER 10

We walked past another one of those mermaid sculptures on our way down to the marina. The air smelled of salt, and sea birds wailed in the distance. It had taken a little while to track down Specialist Edward Morales. Luis and I followed him as he pushed a cart laden with alcohol bottles up the gangplank to a waiting yacht. A red Hawaiian shirt hung loose and open over his t-shirt and shorts. Despite his casual attire, the buzzed brown hair tapering down to his neck marked him as former military.

"Permission to come aboard, sir?" I asked.

He turned with a passive face. "That depends. You don't look like solicitors or bill collectors. Who are you?"

Luis extended his hand. "We're working for Mr. Thomas Anderson. I hear you and he were friends."

I stared at the black hairs on Luis' knuckles— not so different than my night-time visitor.

Morales didn't take Luis' hand, but a smile flashed across his face, and he waved us forward. He smelled of sweat and alcohol, although he was sober. He hadn't showered yet today and it was mid-afternoon.

He began stocking the bar. "You could say we were friends," he said. "I finally took his advice and became a private contractor." He popped open a bottle and motioned at the boat around him. "Best decision I ever made. You want a drink?"

I couldn't help but smile and glanced at Luis. "No, thank you. Maybe another time when we're not working."

Morales nodded. "You really working for Anderson? I assume you're investigating the whole stolen artifact thing."

Luis nodded. "Yes. He hired us to investigate the charges against him."

Morales took a long swig from the brown bottle. "That's surprising. It seems pretty open and shut."

I raised my eyebrows. "You think he's guilty?"

"Oh, yeah! Of course!"

His response was so immediate and certain, it almost caused a laugh to burst from my mouth, but I managed to hold it back. "What makes you so sure?"

"All I did over there was drive a forklift, but I see things. He shipped goods in and out all the time. He was the party guy, the booze supplier. Everyone knew him. No one ever questioned him."

"So despite bases in Iraq being dry, Anderson was able to ship in alcohol?"

"Yup. And pretty much everyone knew it. No one wanted to cut off the good times, so no one looked too closely at his shipments. It was better not to know any specifics so you wouldn't have to lie if anyone asked about it."

"You reported to Captain Nguyen?" I said.

"Yes, sir. Good ol' Captain Nguyen. You should question her. She and Anderson were pretty tight."

"Were they?" I said.

"Oh, yeah. Anderson could get it all: money, booze, hotties."

"Are you referring to your superior as a *hottie*?" I asked.

Morales shrugged. "The service is still 80% men. Standards are different over there."

I had trouble seeing the gruff, professional officer in baggy khakis we had questioned earlier as a *hottie*. "Are you implying Captain Nguyen and Anderson had more than a professional relationship?"

"Yes, sir, they were boning, sir."

I resisted the urge to look at Luis. Not much surprised me these days, but that did. Captain Nguyen didn't seem to have much respect for Anderson when we had spoken earlier. I remembered her saying something about *paying her debts*. "Did you ever bet money in Anderson's games?"

He took another swig from the bottle. "Oh, yeah. I think most of us did at some point."

"Did you owe him money?"

"I won some. I lost some."

"And Captain Nguyen? Did she owe money?"

He shrugged. "I don't know anything about that, but I know she gambled with him and drank his alcohol."

I nodded and felt a weight lift. Perhaps this woman who had the nerve to reference my record during our interview had some skeletons of her own.

"Did you ever hear Anderson talk about artifacts?" I asked.

"Nope," Morales said.

"And did you ever see him with anything that might have been an artifact?"

Morales tried to say *no* while guzzling beer at the same time, "Mm-mmm." He then dropped the bottle in the trash with a satisfying thump. "You sure you don't want a beer or something? I've got a really smooth microbrew here."

I smiled and handed him a card. "No, thank you. Give me a call if you think of anything else."

"Sure." He waved as we walked back down the gangplank. "Good luck," he called after us. "If you're trying to prove Anderson innocent, you're going to need it."

When we rounded a corner, I finally looked at Luis and burst out laughing. After yesterday and this morning, I needed the laugh.

Luis must have read my mind. He did a bad impersonation of me asking, *"Mr. Morales, do you think he's guilty?"*

And I repeated, *"Oh yeah! Of course!"*

We stopped at a nice seafood place for dinner. At least I wouldn't starve on this case. I nibbled rolls and whipped out my tablet while we waited for our entrees. Morales' Instagram account was open to the public. I found pictures of him on his boat drinking and playing games with a host of young women in tiny bathing suits. I doubted his employers would like seeing all that drinking and debauchery on a public page. I was constantly amazed how careless people could be on social media. These photos were available to anyone who bothered to look.

Nguyen's Facebook page had higher privacy settings. I sent a friend request from one of my fake accounts but doubted she would bite. I could still scroll through her public profile pictures. In one, a uniformed Captain Nguyen stood on a towering staircase of mud brick which receded into the sky above her. She smiled and squinted in the bright sunlight with a lowered AK-47 in her hands.

A short internet search revealed the staircase to be part of the Ziggurat of Ur, one of the most ancient temples in the world. Seeing Nguyen brandishing her weapon in uniform on one of Iraq's most sacred sites made me realize how the United States might be seen as invaders and occupiers, but if I'd been there and had the opportunity to walk in the footsteps of Gilgamesh and Enkidu, I wouldn't have passed it up either.

Nguyen certainly knew about Anderson's gambling ring and contraband alcohol. If she wasn't actively helping, she at least turned a blind eye to it. She had access to sacred sites and more direct access to shipping lines than Anderson. If they'd had a romantic relationship, they could have smuggled items out together. Or, if they'd had an argument, she could have motivation to frame him, but I considered that a pretty farfetched idea. Framing Anderson would have been a lot of work with no financial reward. The artifacts were now in the hands of authorities and wouldn't be worth anything to the person who'd taken all the risk getting them here.

# CHAPTER 11

The door swung open, and I stared into a freshly cleaned hotel room. The bed was made and the bathroom smelled of bleach, but it looked exactly like the room I had been in the night before. If my visitor had been real, it might follow some natural rules. It had remained confined in the trashcan. It could have entered through the door when I had opened it. It didn't appear to crawl through solid walls.

After placing my bags and plastic shopping sack on the desk, I inspected the vent above the door and the duct behind it. No one else in the hotel had complained of strange visitations. The smell of roses and charred wood had been the same scent I'd detected around the artifacts in the evidence room. I suspected the hand would be looking specifically for me in whatever room I chose.

*Looking?* How could a hand look for someone when it had no eyes? Maybe it *felt* its way to its victims. The idea of it slowly feeling its way along the walls gave me the creeps.

I reached into the plastic sack and opened the thin boxes within. I then placed the rat traps on the floor around the bed. If the trays of super adhesive glue could stop giant rats, I figured they would at least slow down a disembodied hand. I also placed two glue traps on the tables next to the bed, in case the hand decided to climb up to me that way. If my visitor returned, I would have some definitive evidence it was real.

I decided to try calling Bulsara's office number again. Now that voicemail was full as well. A weak and weary tenor voice answered the home phone.

"Hello!" I said, excited to get a real person. "I'm looking for Aarif Bulsara."

"I'm sorry. He's not here."

"Can you have him call me back?"

"I'm afraid that won't be possible."

"Why?"

"He's dead."

The line clicked. "Hello?" I called. "Hello?" I tried the number again and got the full voicemail message once more.

I turned to the internet once again and found a headline: THIRD HANDLESS BODY FOUND. Bulsara's body had been discovered in a public park early the previous morning with three .32 caliber bullets in his back. He was missing one hand.

I scanned the glue traps surrounding me to make sure they were still free of intruders.

The article said the culprit was a serial killer. I googled the names of two other victims, an archeologist and another professor, both shot in the back with .32 caliber bullets and found without their right hands.

I dialed agent Wittman and told him what I had found.

"The bodies were found in different states, so it is FBI jurisdiction," Wittman said, "but it's someone else's case. I don't see how this relates to the stolen artifacts."

I had left out the part about the latest victim appearing to me in their evidence room and his dismembered hand climbing over my bed. Wittman didn't believe I had really seen anyone in the property room and bringing it up would probably just piss him off. Without that, I didn't actually have anything linking the cases. "I don't either," I said. "Yet. But they have to be connected."

"Call me if you ever find anything concrete." I could hear the skepticism in his voice.

Before he could hang up, I blurted, "Were the hands sliced off, like with an ax, or were they smashed and ripped?"

"What?"

"Was the ulna left a little longer, like the victim had been defending himself when it happened, or was it a straight cut?"

"Like I said, it's not my case. What are you getting at, Mr. Mahler? What does that have to do with stolen artifacts?"

"I'm not sure."

"I'll talk to the agent in charge." He hung up abruptly without another word. He assumed I was nuts, and I couldn't blame him.

I drifted to sleep with the lamp on that night. When the air conditioner kicked on, my eyes shot open, and I scanned the room, but the glue traps remained empty.

Perhaps the hand hadn't been attacking me. Perhaps the ghost was asking for help. But it hadn't acted like a victim in the evidence room, and the hand had jumped for my face the night before. I would have slept better if Alpha and Meega had been with me. The dogs would never let a severed hand sneak up on me.

The only thing I managed to trap that night was my own foot when I got up to use the restroom early the next morning. I re-boxed the glue traps, put them back in the bag and stuffed them in a drawer so they wouldn't freak out the cleaning crew.

The sun wasn't up yet, but I didn't think I'd be getting any more sleep that morning.

# CHAPTER 12

It took me a little over five hours to drive to Lancaster, Pennsylvania, but I never felt like I was far from civilization. Everything felt so much closer on the east coast than back in New Mexico. I had started out before sunrise and hoped to be back to Norfolk before Luis noticed I was gone.

A few photographers waited like vultures outside the domed mosque, hoping to catch a glimpse of the grieving widow. I felt disgusted by them, but I was no better. I'd tried to get to the burial, but the service at the cemetery must have been very short. Everyone was already gone by the time I arrived. At least I could still make this post-burial memorial.

Once through the door, I followed a sign down some steps just within the entrance. Even without the sign, I could have followed the sound of voices and smell of food. Folding chairs were set in rows, and a line of about forty people marched past the family offering condolences. Other than the Arabic calligraphy on the wall, this room was not unlike any of the other multipurpose community rooms in Christian churches across the country.

The family stood surrounded by photographs of Aarif Bulsara. He beamed for the camera with his new bride, laughed with his baby girl, scored a soccer goal, lectured at a podium. His brother and sister told stories in front of the assembled friends and family. They made the family laugh through their tears. Aarif Bulsara now felt like a real person to me, not just a clue or a name in the newspaper. The brother had a vague resemblance, but there were no surprise twins waiting to explain my apparition in the FBI property room.

Among the sea of older faces, a group of four young people, possibly the victim's students, congregated in the corner.

My phone vibrated in my pocket, and I knew it was Luis asking where I was. I texted back that I was following up a lead. When it vibrated again, I ignored it. There was no point in being here if I spent the whole time staring at my phone.

The widow Bulsara wore a black headscarf. I shook her hand. The brother hovered close by as though guarding her. "I'm sorry for your loss," I said. "Are there any leads on who did this?"

The weary voice I'd heard on the phone yesterday said, "Thank you. No. It wouldn't change anything anyway. It wouldn't bring him back. How did you know Aarif?"

I had intended to tell the truth, but in the moment, I lied. "He was helping me interpret some inscriptions on Iraqi artifacts."

"Are you a linguist too?" she asked.

"No. I'm an investigator. The artifacts were stolen from Iraq. He didn't mention anything about them?"

"No."

"That's surprising. It was an interesting case. I hate to ask at such a time, but if he has any notes, I'd really like to take a look at them."

She pointed at a man by the door. His silver hair was as long as mine but not tied back. "Talk to Dr. Speiser. Any notes would be in Aarif's office at the university."

"Thank you."

I felt dirty lying to her, and the lie might make it more difficult if I needed to follow up with her later. If I'd been able to talk to her at another time, I would have been honest, but interrogating her at her husband's memorial made me feel no better than the photographers outside. It hadn't been a complete lie. Something or someone with Aarif Bulsara's face had talked to me about the artifacts. The real Bulsara would have already been dead at the time. Perhaps it was his ghost.

"Dr. Speiser," I called. The silver-haired man turned his wire rimmed glasses my way. "Mrs. Bulsara suggested I talk to you." I decided to use the victim's first name to create a sense that I had been familiar with him. "I had been talking to Aarif about some inscriptions, and she said his notes were in his office at the university."

"If you come by tomorrow morning, around 9 a.m., we can look for them."

I winced. "I'm afraid I wasn't planning to be in town that long." I paused and lowered my voice. "I didn't want to mention this, but I think something he was working on could have been what got him killed."

Speiser took a step back. "What did you say your name was?"

I handed him a card. "Jack Mahler."

A short, pudgy man approached. Through a bite of falafel, he asked, "Did I hear you say you were working with Aarif on some inscriptions?" Bushy eyebrows arched over his eyes. His small plate smelled delicious. I already felt like an intruder and had been too ashamed to dare take any food.

I noticed the flat, round hat over his thinning hair. "Is that a yarmulke?"

The man had a very slight accent on some of his vowels that I couldn't place. "It is."

"I didn't expect to see a Jewish person at a Muslim memorial."

He smiled. "I didn't expect to see so many gentiles."

"Touché! I just meant, with all the history—"

"I know what you meant, but our people haven't always been enemies, and we have more in common than we have differences." He gazed at the widow and the photos beside her. "Especially here, in America, where we are both minorities." The man turned back to me and extended his hand. "I am Rabbi Benaiah Chesniak. People call me Ben."

While Ben was talking, Dr. Speiser wandered away and was already involved in another conversation.

The rabbi drew my attention back to him. "Aarif had called me for some help with these Akkadian and Canaanite inscriptions."

"Really!" I whipped out my phone and showed the photo of the faded scratches inside the stolen ring. "Something like that?" The rabbi squinted at the screen, and I apologized for the image quality. "I'm sorry the photo isn't very clear."

Ben shrugged, blinked and looked away from the screen. "Unfortunately, by the time I made it down here, Aarif had already disappeared. I never got a chance to see what he was working on."

"Damn!"

The rabbi cocked his head and arched an eyebrow.

"Sorry." I corrected myself, "Darn."

Ben smiled. "It sounds like this project was very important to you."

I tried to explain myself without sounding crazy. "I'm investigating some stolen artifacts that were taken from the Iraq Museum. I think Aarif was working on something related to them."

Ben's thick eyebrows lifted. "And you think that somehow got him killed?"

I sucked in a deep breath. "I do." I started grasping for some rational motivation that didn't sound insane. "Maybe the thief had hired him to translate the inscriptions."

"That would be a very scholarly thief."

A long pause hung between us.

I finally said in a whisper, "He's not the only academic to be killed."

The rabbi's voice became equally quiet. "I know." We paused again. He finally continued, "Archaeolinguistics is a relatively small field. We all knew each other on some level, even if it was just seeing each other at annual conferences."

I wasn't sure what to say, so I put a hand on the rabbi's shoulder in an attempt to be comforting.

He smiled. "I'm planning to visit Aarif's office tomorrow," the rabbi finally said. "Speiser asked me to organize his notes and books. Would you like to meet me there in the morning? Perhaps we can discover what he was working on."

Luis might kill me for spending another night and day chasing this long shot, and I'd left my luggage back in Norfolk, but this might be my only chance to find out if Aarif was really connected to the stolen artifacts. It wouldn't be the first time I'd worn the same clothes two days in a row. Hell, for nine years I never worried about clothes. "Sure, I'll meet you there." I remembered seeing some cheap motels by the interstate.

"In the meantime," Ben said, "are you doing anything for dinner? There's a kosher deli near my hotel."

I glanced at the empty plate in the rabbi's hand.

"Only an appetizer," he said.

# CHAPTER 13

I left the mosque and checked my phone. The phone call hadn't been from Luis. It had been Diane. I looked up Rabbi Benaiah Chesniak. He taught at Emory University in Atlanta, Georgia. For such an unassuming fellow, he had a long list of PhDs.

I returned Diane's call.

"How is the case going?" she asked.

"I've run around and talked to a lot of people, but all I've really learned is that Anderson is a creep, which I already knew."

"Well, you must be ruffling some feathers. An FBI agent came to the office asking about you."

"Wow, I must have really pissed them off in the evidence room."

"What did you do, Jack?"

"Don't say it like that! It's like you expect me to screw up."

"No, but I know how you can be a smartass at the worst times."

"Well, this time it wasn't that. I saw something they didn't, and now they think I'm crazy."

"What did you see?"

"Apparently I had a conversation with an invisible man in their locked evidence room."

Diane remained quiet for a moment. "Maybe the man had gotten into the room somehow without being seen."

"Luis and an FBI agent were with me when I had this whole conversation, and they didn't see a thing."

Diane became silent again.

"You think I'm crazy too."

"I've always known you were crazy, Jack. That's part of your charm. This is a little weird though, even for you."

If she thought I was weird now, I wondered how Diane would react if she knew the whole story about my missing nine years. "What did the agent ask about me?"

"Mostly character questions, like how well I knew you, what kind of person you are, how your work ethic is, if you like to travel."

"That's all?"

"They wanted to know what specific cases you'd worked on, but I told them they'd need a warrant for that kind of information."

I knew Wittman thought I was crazy and maybe even a jerk, but I was surprised he considered me worth sending someone to conduct interviews. They'd already run an extensive background check on me.

"There's something else I wanted to talk about, Jack. Meega still isn't eating."

"Still! I shouldn't have left her so soon after the incident with Animal Control."

"I'm taking her to the vet tomorrow."

"You think it's a physical illness? She always eats less when I leave town."

"It's probably nothing, Jack, but I'd rather be sure."

"Save the bill. I'll reimburse you when I'm back in town."

"It's alright, Jack. This is for my own piece of mind more than anything. I'm sure it's nothing, but I wanted to let you know."

"Thanks, Diane. Meega and Alpha are my family. They consider you and Reece family too. I know they're in good hands."

I dreaded calling Luis, but I had to tell him I'd be gone overnight. Considering I had never told him I was coming here in the first place, that wasn't going to sit well. He took it better than I feared.

"I know you are used to working on your own," he said, "but this is supposed to be a team effort, Jack. I didn't come all the way here for a vacation. I've got other things I could be doing right now back home."

I wanted to ask what he had to do that was so important. Take Diane to more dinners? Practice his golf swing while Diane did his job for him? In a rare instance of wisdom, I decided to stay quiet.

"Your methods are eccentric," he continued, "but you've gotten results in the past. We're running out of leads here anyway. I can't authorize the expense of the motel in Lancaster, though. We're already paying for your room here."

I tried to argue. "I didn't plan on staying the night."

"It wouldn't look right. Anderson might not notice the double billing, but you can bet his lawyer would. That would invite her to examine every little expense."

There was no arguing with that, but I still felt Luis was trying to punish me for leaving without telling him.

\* \* \*

Ben sipped his coffee. "Sargon was a fascinating character, the most famous king most modern people have never heard of. He built a massive temple and created one of the first expansive empires ranging from the Mediterranean all the way to the Persian Gulf. It became the model all other empires would be compared to for millennia after his death. To top it all off, he supposedly didn't start out as any kind of royalty. Legend says he started out as a gardener."

"Wow! How did he go from gardener to the most powerful man in the world?"

"Details about the real Sargon are thin. We don't even know for sure if Sargon was his birth name. The name translates as *Confirmed King— Sarru* meaning *king*.

"Sarru-Kin."

"Yes! Exactly! Legends say he was found as a baby in a river like Moses and that he commanded spirits to build his great temple like the stories of King Solomon 2,000 years later."

"I remember stories about King Solomon being super wise, but I've never heard anything about commanding spirits."

"According to Jewish tradition and legends that sprang up in the Middle Ages, Solomon had all kinds of powers. He could talk to animals and to the dead. He rode all over the world on the back of an eagle or on a magic carpet."

"A magic carpet? Like Aladdin and the genie?"

"Very much like Aladdin and the genie of the ring! In fact, in the Islamic tradition, the spirits and demons Solomon commanded were said to be jinn— what you would call genies. They were forced to obey him because he had the secret name of God inscribed on his ring of power."

"Ring of power?" I whipped out the photo of the ring and the inscription. "Like this one?"

Ben lifted his right hand, revealing a silver ring. The disk on its face was decorated with a six-pointed star. "More like this one, but the principal is the same. The inscription on the ring in your photo could be a spell of protection."

"Or the name of a god…?"

"Or guardian spirit, yes. But of course those are all just legends."

I'd discovered other legends with foundations in reality. I gazed down at the image. "A legend may not always be real, but it can still motivate real people to real action."

Ben nodded, suddenly excited. "They can indeed! Look at the hunts for the Holy Grail, or the Spear of Destiny or, since we mentioned him earlier, King Solomon's mines!"

I pointed at the image on my phone again. "Can you actually read this stuff?"

Ben slipped on some reading glasses. "Tsu… Tsu…Tsukal… Part of it is obscured. I'm not sure whether it's the image quality or the wear on the artifact itself."

"Sorry about that. Unfortunately the museum didn't provide any photos of the insides of the rings. No one speaks this language anymore, right?"

"Oh, no, not for thousands of years."

"But you were reading it out loud. How do you know how to say the words?"

"Proper names are harder, but I have a rough approximation of how the syllables sounded in other words that had similarities to known languages."

"So you can say the words the way people said them back then?"

"Well, let's say it's not impossible, but exact pronunciation is unlikely. Aarif believed that pronunciations changed at regular intervals, dropping certain consonants on the ends of the words, adding vowels to the beginnings, things like that. He claimed you could determine original pronunciations by tracing these changes backward. He even believed he could discover an original language spoken by all humans before the Tower of Babel. But, if these regular intervals even exist at all, there are too many other variables affecting them— influences from other cultures and languages for example."

"The more I learn, the more certain I am that there is no possible way to know how a word was pronounced 4,000 years ago."

"That may not be completely true. We have clues. We can look at cognates in more modern Semitic languages like Arabic and Hebrew."

"Wait, I thought Semitic meant Jewish. Are you saying it applies to Arabs too?"

"It refers to their languages. In the late nineteenth century Semitic began to be used more specifically for Jews with the term *anti-Semitic*." Ben shook his head with a look of sadness in his eyes. "Ah, the ever evolving language."

I almost regretted asking, but asking questions was the only way to learn.

Fortunately, Ben got back on track. "The modern pronunciation for the name Sargon, for example, was taken from a reference to a much later king named Sargon referred to in the Bible."

I raised my eyebrows. "But I had heard him called *Sarrukin*, and even a name that started with an *L,* which sounds completely different."

"Exactly! The modern pronunciation only used the one source! But there are other clues we can use. Spelling wasn't as consistent in the time before moveable type and spell check. We can compare ancient graffiti to other words and syllables in official documents."

"Graffiti?"

"Yes! Look at modern graffiti and tell me it doesn't read more like we talk. I've got these fancy degrees, but the linguists of the future could learn more about the way we talk by reading the walls in the inner cities than anything I've ever written."

"Unless they've got audio tape."

Ben chuckled a bit at that. "Of course! Unfortunately, King Sargon didn't record any audio tapes as far as we know."

I smiled and repeated, "As far as we know."

"Along with graffiti, we've got texts written by non-native speakers who spelled things like they sounded in their own languages, and some of those languages are known today. We can also find words and syllables in poetry to see how they fit the rhythm and rhyme of the words around it."

"So if you do all of that, it will tell you the correct pronunciation?"

"*All of that* is an arduous process that could take a lifetime. Assuming we are able to find all of those variations I mentioned, we can determine a list of possibilities, and one of those possibilities should be the proper pronunciation, but you are correct that it is nearly impossible to know which of those variations is exactly how the word was originally spoken."

I shook my head. "So after all that, you get one correct multiple choice answer with no answer key."

"Exactly!"

# CHAPTER 14

Even with semis pounding along the interstate just outside my window, I awoke more refreshed than I had the last couple of days. I didn't know if there was any reason a dead man's hand couldn't find me in a different city or a different building, but the little motel room still felt more secure. I'd done a quick, soapy rinse of my shirt and socks in the sink the night before and had left them hanging above the shower. They were dry enough.

Kids shuffled between ivy-covered buildings at Franklin & Marshall College. Seeing how young they all looked made me feel old. I'd lost nine years of my life, but I had still aged all that time I was missing. University life was foreign to me. Mom would have preferred I go to a place like this, but instead I went straight from high school into the Army. I wanted to be a hero like my dad. I became a disgrace instead.

The campus wasn't huge, but it still took me a while to find the Department of Ancient History, and then I had to find the right office. Even with the delay, I was 20 minutes early, so I took a short walk to rid myself of nervous energy. The campus was so green that it felt like walking in a park. When I got back, I found the door open. The office was much bigger than I had expected but cluttered with papers and file cabinets. A bookshelf covered one wall.

Ben sat at a long table, pouring over stacks of paper and books. "Ah, Jack." He pulled out an enlarged, high-resolution photo of cuneiform writing. "This is what Aarif was working on before he disappeared." The letters curved along a round surface. Three rows and a partial fourth were visible in the photo, much more than would fit on a small finger ring.

I whipped out the image on my phone. "Is any of it the same?"

"No, but there are words missing before and after where the photo cuts off. The sequence repeats, shifting to the right below." He ran his finger along the letters. "Obey… king…"

I scooted a chair out and sat beside him. If the inscription had matched, it would have meant a possible connection between the deaths and Anderson's stolen artifacts. Perhaps this really was all unconnected, and this side trip had been a waste of time.

A voice echoed from the doorway. "Rabbi Chesniak! And Jack Mahler! What a surprise!" A portly, broad-shouldered man in a white suit shook my hand, and I looked up from the table, confused. The man was tall as well as broad. A jet-black goatee, probably dyed, decorated his chin, but his head was polished to a hairless shine. "I was hoping for a chance to meet the man with the strange questions in person."

The accent and face finally clicked. "Jules Castor, the antiquities dealer?" I'd never met him in person, so I didn't have a smell to identify him with. All I had was an internet image and a brief, late night phone call.

"Appraiser would be a better title for me," Castor said. "Someone else handles the selling."

Ben stood and shook Castor's hand.

"You know each other?" I asked.

"From the memorial," Castor said.

"That's where we met as well," I said.

"When I found out what had happened to Aarif and the others, I had to come. Such a tragedy!" He noticed the photo on the table and put on tiny round spectacles. "Is that what Aarif had been working on? Where is it from?"

"I'm not sure," Ben said, scanning over the books and papers. "But I believe I will eventually trip over the full inscription in one of these books."

"Can I get a copy of this photo?" I asked. "Maybe the other victims were working on something similar."

Castor nodded. "A good idea."

"Of course." Ben took the photo from the room.

Castor took the rabbi's chair and leaned in close. "Did you and Chesniak arrive here together this morning?"

"He beat me by a few minutes. Why?"

"You know I've worked with the FBI in the past. I consider myself a bit of an amateur sleuth. I could not stay away from something like this. Don't you think it a little suspicious that Rabbi Chesniak knew all the victims? And now he is so eager to be the first to clean Aarif's office!"

"Are you implying Rabbi Chesniak had something to do with the deaths?"

"I'm just saying it is suspicious. A Jew is always looking for an advantage."

That last part shocked me. "You're saying he's suspicious because he is Jewish?"

"I'm saying he is suspicious because he knew all the victims. With them gone, he now is the world's foremost authority on these inscriptions. Tell me, Jack, what brought you to this case? Did one of the victim's families hire you?"

I hesitated, unsure how to answer. "No. I thought there might be a connection between the deaths and the stolen Iraqi artifacts."

Castor's eyes swelled with surprise and intensity. "Really! What makes you think that?"

I shook my head. "I don't know. Just a crazy hunch, I guess." I looked at the stacks of books around us. "Maybe it was stupid."

"No! No. Anything is possible, and there is certainly a missing piece to this puzzle. I have more experience in these matters. Maybe I can find a connection. Where are you staying?"

I gave him the name of my hotel in Norfolk as the rabbi returned. Castor eyed Ben's finger as he handed me copies of the photo.

"That is a beautiful ring," Castor said. "What does it symbolize?"

"Thank you. It is a replica of King Solomon's ring of wisdom."

Castor shot a glance at me, as if to say that meant something, but I wasn't sure what he was trying to imply. Ben had been so kind and personable, but I'd been fooled before by a friendly smile. I was relying on his translation of the photo and analysis of this office's contents, but if he couldn't be trusted, none of this would mean anything.

Chesniak pointed out an inscription on the side of his ring. "Unlike the ring of power, the ring of wisdom didn't have any magic. All it had was one simple reminder: *This too shall pass.* Whether you are on top of the world and feel like you can do no wrong, or you've hit bottom and want to die, this too shall pass."

Castor nodded. "Very wise. These are dark days for us, but they shall pass. Whoever killed these good people should keep those words in mind. They may be in the shadows for now, but the light of day shall hit them soon enough and everyone will know their name."

Even though the office was larger than I had expected, with three of us inside, I began to feel claustrophobic. If a connection did sit in that room, I wouldn't have the knowledge to recognize it. I gave both men my business card and took my leave.

I called the other victims' families using the Bluetooth in the rental car. I struck out with one, but I was able to get hold of the archeologist's husband. When I asked if he knew Chesniak, he talked about how nice the rabbi had been since the murder. Chesniak had even offered to help sort through the victim's belongings in her office.

Was he really being nice, or was he after some secret knowledge? I almost wished Castor hadn't planted that seed in my mind, but I couldn't let myself make any assumptions.

When I arrived back at the hotel in Norfolk, I used the business center to fax the photo to the archeologist's husband and then emailed it to agent Wittman at the FBI as well.

When I got to my room, I barely had time to shower before a knock came at the door. I cautiously peeked out the peep hole to make sure it was a real person and not another bodiless hand. To my surprise, it was Agent Wittman. I grabbed a shirt and invited him in.

He glanced around the room before focusing on me. "I suppose you know why I'm here."

I could only think of one possible reason. I became excited and stopped buttoning my shirt. "Did you find a connection between the artifacts and the murders?"

"What made you ask me about the way the hands were cut?"

I hesitated for a moment, wondering what he was getting at. "It seemed like a natural question."

"Perhaps it should be, but it's not. The general public assumes it was a straight on chop, hacked off by a sharp, heavy blade or sawed off. You are the only person to ask about the angle." He stared at me, not threateningly, but just stood and stared.

That's when I realized he thought I might be involved in the murders somehow. "Well, I am a private investigator."

Wittman continued to stare.

"So, I was right about the angle? The bones were like... smashed off, or something, at a defensive angle?"

He continued to stare. It's a great tactic, just waiting, letting the silence hang until the person you are questioning feels compelled to fill it, sometimes spilling useful information in the process. I could never keep my mouth shut long enough to use that method effectively, but Wittman was a master.

"I haven't left New Mexico for two years," I said. "I mean, until now."

"We know. Rather, we've confirmed you've been in and around Albuquerque for the last month. So the question remains, how did you know how the hands were severed?"

I silently kicked myself. Mentioning an alibi before being asked made me look like I had something to hide. That's when I noticed movement along the floor. Fingers felt their way along the baseboard, seeming to use the wall as a guide as the grotesque hand felt its way from the bathroom and around the corner next to the bed. Sympathetic pain knotted my own hand as the intruder inched forward finger by finger. I felt the blood drain from my face.

I wanted to point at it and shout, *There! That is how I knew!* But when Wittman turned his face to follow my gaze, I clapped my hands causing him to jerk his head back to me. A few minutes ago, I would have loved for someone official to witness the hand and tell me I wasn't crazy, but now that I knew I was a suspect, I wasn't so keen on him finding a victim's severed appendage in my hotel room.

Now that I had Wittman's attention again, I had to say something. "I get... feelings sometimes."

He narrowed his eyes. "Are you trying to tell me you are some sort of psychic detective?"

I forced my eyes to remain on him, trying not to look down at the floor. "No!" I said, although it made as much sense as anything might to him. I'd had a conversation with a man who wasn't there, and I could smell and hear things others seemed oblivious to, like an extra sense. "Just... a strong intuition."

"Despite what you see on television, the Bureau does not employ psychics, Mr. Mahler. I assure you any publicity you might be looking for will backfire. You have some skeletons I'm sure you wouldn't want to resurface."

My whole body seemed to deflate, and I let my eyes fall back to the floor. Wittman followed my gaze. Wherever the hand had gotten to, it wasn't visible. Faint rosewater and smoky wood did nothing to cover the smell of rotten flesh. How could Wittman not smell it? I continued to stare, wondering where it had hidden itself. If the ghost in the evidence room hadn't been visible, would Wittman have been able to see the hand, even if he had stared straight at it?

"It was a logical question, Agent Wittman. That's all."

Wittman took one last glance around the sparse room and my bag hanging open on the bed. "At the moment, the only thing

I see connecting these two cases, is you." He paused, waiting for a response from me.

"I just want to help."

"We'll have our eyes on you, Mr. Mahler."

He didn't bother to close the door behind him, and I stared into the open hallway. I wondered if he would be less suspicious and more appreciative if not for the scandal attached to my name.

I looked under the little end table and sniffed under the bed, but the putrescence had diffused throughout the corner of the room, and the phantom hand, if it existed at all, remained hidden.

# CHAPTER 15

The elevator dinged. I met Luis in the lobby, and we headed to the hotel restaurant. A broad-shouldered man in a rumpled, powder blue suit jacket lifted a newspaper over his face as I passed, leaving only the top of his white hair exposed. The movement of the newspaper, rather than hide him, drew my attention, and I managed to get a peek at a long scar below one eye as I passed. He reminded me of a thug out of a low budget 1950s detective movie. He smelled faintly of sweat but didn't stink. He smelled like a man who worked outdoors rather than someone who'd been working out at a gym.

I would have expected Wittman and the FBI to use a more subtle tail than that, but it wouldn't be the first time Wittman had surprised me. I considered confronting the guy, but figured Wittman would simply replace him with someone more difficult to spot, so I let him be. At the end of the day, the FBI didn't have anything on me.

My biggest fault with Wittman hadn't been my question about the hand; it had just been annoying him in the property room, which made me look like a stupid jerk, but not like a criminal. I didn't think that was worth all this effort— talking to my friends and coworkers, paying someone to follow me around— especially after they'd confirmed I wasn't anywhere near the murders. Apparently, Wittman thought it was a justified use of our tax money.

Our government at work.

Luis continued to talk while he chewed his steak. "You can't be working an unrelated case and charging the expenses to our client. These murders might be more interesting to you, but we need to stay focused on the Anderson case, no matter how you feel about it."

"What else do we have to go on? We're out of leads."

"Let's just for a moment consider the possibility that our client really didn't take those artifacts."

"Then someone else had to have done it."

"Exactly," Luis said. "Who?"

"Someone who had access to his storage unit? Someone who had access to the artifacts? Why go to all that trouble? Were they planning to sell them out of another person's storage unit? Using his email address? What if Anderson had found them and either called the authorities or, more likely, sold them himself. Were they willing to risk losing them all?"

"Those artifacts were priceless!" Luis exclaimed. "After all the trouble they went through to get them here, there is no way they would give them up."

"Unless it wasn't for money," I wondered aloud.

"What else could it have been?"

I shook my head. "I don't know. Cultural knowledge? Cool keepsakes?"

"That's a lot of risk for a keepsake."

"You are the one who wanted to go down this path. The simplest explanation is that Anderson really took them."

"Maybe. But we need to explore other possibilities. It's our job."

I wanted to scream that it was *his* job, not mine, but I held myself in check. "If anyone other than Anderson had the opportunity and resources to steal those artifacts and then sneak them into Anderson's storage unit, it would be Zachary King or someone who worked for him at Strateegis. He had almost complete freedom of movement in Iraq at that time."

"Thanks to you, I doubt King will agree to another meeting with us. While you took a vacation in Pennsylvania, I poured over King's report looking for discrepancies and comparing it to the list of witnesses the FBI gave us. We can try talking to some of the Strateegis people who worked with Anderson. What about the woman, Captain Nguyen? People in love don't always act rationally."

"Maybe. Ask Anderson who else had access to his unit."

"I think you should be the one to ask him."

I again held myself in check, but I couldn't stop myself from glaring.

"He specifically hired you, Jack. He doesn't want to see me. I spent most of my last visit assuring him you were working the case. Think of it as revenge, if you like. You get to see him behind bars."

\* \* \*

Even confined within four cinderblock walls and wearing an orange jumpsuit, Anderson swung onto the chair as though he owned the place. The silver table reflected the lights, and the walls were pristine, nothing like the grimy, makeshift prison we had managed back in Afghanistan. His jumpsuit smelled freshly laundered. He wasn't sitting in his own filth like the men we had guarded.

I sat across from him. "Why didn't you tell us you were sleeping with Captain Nguyen?"

"Didn't seem relevant." He winked. "And we didn't do much sleeping."

"Damn it, Anderson, anything could be relevant!"

"She may not look like much in the civilian world, but in the service?" Anderson nodded his head, and the corner of his mouth lifted in a crooked smile. "Did she tell you about it? Did she say it was good?"

I released a frustrated breath. "No. She didn't mention it at all, but she did say you were guilty."

"What?"

"Morales said the same thing."

Anderson's face reddened. "He would never say that. They're my friends."

I tapped my finger on the table, remembering how he had once expected me to lie for him out of friendship. "I'm starting to think you don't have any real friends."

"That's not true. I give Morales a hard time occasionally, but he knows it's all in fun." Anderson folded his arms over his chest. "And I've got you."

I don't know how long I let my mouth hang open. "You can't be serious."

"Of course I'm serious! You took the fall for me all those years ago, and you're helping me now. You're my hero, Jackie—Jack. You'll swoop in to save the day. It's what you do."

Did he really think I was his friend, or was he trying to manipulate me somehow? "I am not your friend, Anderson. I've spent the last eleven years cursing your name!"

He furrowed his brow, mouth half open, and stared at me. I almost felt bad for him before I remembered who I was talking to.

"Who else had access to your storage unit?" I asked.

"Only me."

"Are you sure?"

"And my mom."

"That's what I'm talking about! You can't leave out shit like that!"

"But my mom wouldn't stash artifacts in my unit! How would she even have gotten them?"

"You can be sure the prosecutor will have a few theories. Maybe she was your accomplice in the States. Did you send the artifacts to your mom and have her move them for you?"

"My elderly mom?"

"Millions of dollars could set an elderly woman up in a luxurious facility for the rest of her life."

"That's my mom you're talking about! You think she loaded the artifacts into the basket on her walker one at a time?"

"Maybe she hired a mover?"

I handed him a list of the dates and times his code had been used to get into the storage facility. "Looks like you didn't visit your unit too often."

"No." He pointed at a date two years ago. "That was when I bought that sofa and matching love seat. I got a good deal on them and thought I'd need them when I eventually moved into a permanent place of my own, but I never settled down. I could have bought ten sets of new furniture with all the money I've paid renting that storage unit."

"But then what would you have done with all your old cassettes?"

Anderson smiled. "Should have gotten rid of those I suppose. I listen to all the music I want online now, but those cassettes are my youth, man! When you move as much as I do, you want at least one place that is stable."

He shook his head and handed the paper back. "None of these other times in the last year were me. I wasn't even in the country the last two times."

"Well, that's something I can verify, at least."

I stood up abruptly and banged on the door for the guard to let me out.

"Thanks, Jack," Anderson said. "Buddy."

That last word made me want to scream, but I stared straight ahead as the guard opened the door.

I was still fuming as I left the prison. Could the man I've been cursing for eleven years actually be so stupid that he thinks we are friends? Is that how he gets through life treating people like crap? By telling himself it is some sort of good-natured ribbing?

# CHAPTER 16

The wide hallways of Saint Andrews Assisted Living center smelled of fried chicken. Dinner was being served in the attached cafeteria, and I realized I hadn't eaten since breakfast. Soft, warm light lit walls decorated with textured paint and photos of old boats and lighthouses. I found a door with a sign that read, *Home Sweet Home,* but no one answered when I knocked, and I couldn't hear any movement within.

A key jangled against a walker with heavy-duty wheels and a wire basket. The woman paused her slow march through the corridor and asked, "May I help you?" Her voice was strong, despite her age. She wore her silver hair permed into a wave. Soft powder and pink lipstick decorated a face with fewer wrinkles than I might have expected. My mom would have been the same age if she were still alive.

I opened my mouth to introduce myself, but she stopped me, saying, "Wait," and letting her mouth hang open. "Jack Mahler?"

I paused, stunned. "Yes."

Her mouth stretched into a smile as she unlocked the door. "Come in! I'm just getting back from dinner."

The clean, orderly room within smelled like baby powder. A small kitchenette lay off to the side as soon as we walked in. Glass double doors let unfiltered sunlight shine on a couch and chair which sat in front of a small, flat-screen television.

"Can I get you some coffee?" she asked. "Tommy gave me this fancy single-serving coffee maker. I have some cookies in the freezer. They stay fresher that way."

On one wall hung a big photo of a smiling Sergeant Anderson in dress uniform. On the table next to the couch was a photo of Anderson with his arm around me. We were both smiling. I didn't remember that photo being taken. The only photo I remembered from those days was the one I wanted to forget.

"It's so good to finally meet you in person," she said. "Tommy talks about you all the time. Tommy and Jackie back in the good ol' days."

I accepted a plate of crisp, freezing cookies while the smell of coffee filled the small room. She lowered herself onto the easy chair. "It's so rare for any of Tommy's friends to drop by anymore."

I sat on the couch next to her and realized I still hadn't said a word. "It's… good to meet you too," I finally said. "Tommy talks about me?"

"Oh, yes! You must have had quite a time over there! I bet you have some good stories about my Tommy too."

I tried to smile, but my lips were tight. "You could say that."

Liquid swished in the kitchenette. "Coffee's done." She started to lift herself from the chair.

"I can get it," I said, rising, but she was already up and back to the walker.

"Nonsense! You are my guest. My legs are fine. I only need the walker for balance."

I sat back as she fiddled with the machine.

"Do you know why I'm here, Mrs. Anderson?"

"It's Betty!" she demanded. Two coffee mugs sat on a tray attached to the walker and she handed me one. "You don't need any reason to visit!"

"You know Tommy…" I couldn't believe how quickly I fell into using her nomenclature. "Your son is in prison."

"Prison? That can't be. Why would they put my sweet Tommy in prison?"

*Sweet Tommy?* She couldn't be serious. Did her son really not tell her? Perhaps she had dementia. I explained, "He's been accused of stealing Iraqi artifacts."

"That's ridiculous."

"He hired my agency to try and prove he didn't do it."

She nodded. "Oh good! If anyone can do it, you can. My boy's in good hands with you, Jackie."

"The artifacts were stashed in his storage unit. I need to know who had his code."

"His code?"

"To get in the gate to the storage unit."

"Oh," She rotated her head around, scanning the room. "I've got that around here somewhere."

"Who else had it?"

"Oh, I don't know."

"Did you give it to anyone? Ask someone to move something in or out for you?"

"Do you need the key to the unit? I have that in a drawer in the kitchen."

"Key? It was a combination lock."

"Oh, no. I'm not good at remembering numbers."

This was getting me nowhere. I thought about telling her what a creep her son was. It didn't seem fair. Anderson's mom was alive and well. She thought her boy was the greatest thing in the world and that I was his friend. My mom had died not knowing whether I was alive or dead. I'd never have the chance to show her I was anything more than a disgraced failure.

It wasn't my place to shatter this woman's vision of her son. If I could have given my own mother a lie like this, it would have been much better than the truth.

I set my mug down and got up to leave. "Thank you for your time, Mrs. Anderson."

"I told you, it's Betty. You come by any time, darlin.'"

On my way to the door, I noticed several phone numbers written on a magnetic dry-erase board stuck to a half-sized refrigerator. Along with the phone numbers was a five digit number. "Betty," I said. "Is that the code to the storage unit?"

"Hmm? Oh, yes, I think that might be it."

I let out an exasperated breath. Anyone who came into the room could have seen it and figured out what it was.

"Did any other friends of your son come by for a visit?"

"Oh, not for quite a while."

"Anyone specific you could tell me about? An old girlfriend perhaps?"

The corner of her mouth lifted, just like Anderson's does when he's about to get inappropriate. "Oh, no. He never brought any of his girlfriends by. I keep asking when he's going to make me some grandbabies, but no woman can ever tie my Tommy down for long."

# CHAPTER 17

Nguyen stood on a ladder repairing the gutters of a two-story colonial house with powder blue siding. Her hair was still wound into a tight braid. In her denim cutoff shorts and thin white tank top, I could see how Anderson and Morales could find the voluptuous woman attractive.

A German shepherd lay beneath the ladder. Its ears tilted forward, and it growled as I approached.

"Captain Nguyen?" I called.

"Well, look who's been practicing his pronunciation."

When I continued forward, the dog tensed and the hair stood up on her back.

"Careful," Nguyen said. "She bites."

I squatted slowly to my knees with my head just above the dog's height and released a barely audible growl of my own. The dog scooted back with a lowered head. I let out a high-pitched whine and slowly reached out with an upraised palm. She sniffed me, and I scratched her head, allowing her to brush her nose against me.

"I've got to get these gutters fixed before the storm sets in." Nguyen climbed down and saw me petting her dog. "I've never seen her do that before!"

The dog leaned against my leg as I stood to face Nguyen. I didn't bother with niceties. "Is it true you had a sexual relationship with Anderson?"

Nguyen's eyes grew wide, and she looked to the house, possibly worried someone inside might hear. "What if I did? I had sex with a lot of people when I was deployed. That was there and this is here."

It appeared Nguyen considered the two parts of her life to be disconnected, almost like she had two completely separate identities. I motioned my head toward the door to the house. "Would whoever is inside the house feel the same way?"

She narrowed her eyes. "You're trespassing, and my shotgun is just inside the door. What do you want?"

At the mention of her gun, I felt the lack of weight on my left side where my pistol usually rested. "How long were you dating Anderson?"

"We never dated!" She insisted. "We just had sex a couple of times."

"Did you participate in Anderson's gambling ring?"

"I played a few times, but it was a waste of time and money."

"Did you owe him money?"

"A little. I paid it all."

"In cash or…?"

She shook her head. "He may have written off some of my debt after a night of fun."

"I bet that really made you angry— being forced to have sex with him."

I was surprised when a smile of polished white teeth grew along her face. I'd never seen her do anything but scowl. "I've never been forced to do anything in my life. Your views on female sexuality are way out of date. Women have needs too. I did it because I wanted to. I was drunk, happy, horny, and he was convenient."

"But in the conference room you said you resented how he got paid more for the same work—"

"I told you I had sex with him. I never said I respected him. What? Did you think he broke my heart and I got mad and framed him or something? Were you actually going to try to pin his crime on me?"

I opened my mouth, but for once I had no words.

"You are an idiot."

I inhaled and released a tired, resigned breath. "On that, we do agree. Did you ever meet Anderson's mom?"

She seemed to relax a little bit on hearing me admit to my own stupidity. "No. Why would I?"

I kept pulling at strings, but I felt like I was trying to unravel a sweater by tugging on a sock. "How well did you know Edward Morales?"

"Who?"

"Specialist Edward Morales. He was in your company in Iraq, said he drove a forklift…"

"Oh, yes, I remember. He was in line to become a sergeant but had a couple demerits on his record. He could have gotten back on track but decided not to re-up when his contract was up."

I nodded my head. I had been in line to be a sergeant too, the same rank my dad had held, before I got dishonorably discharged. Things hadn't gone the way I'd planned. Unlike Morales, I didn't have a nice job waiting for me on the other side.

At least Nguyen was being a little more forthcoming. Finding out just how incompetent I was must have made her feel more comfortable and less threatened.

"Did you ever see Morales and Anderson hanging out together?" I asked.

"Morales was usually tagging along somewhere in Anderson's shadow. The kid didn't have much taste in friends."

I apologized for my earlier tone and thanked her for her time. "I'm just doing my job," I said.

She shook her head. "Maybe you should look for a better line of work."

I thought about the apparitions I'd seen and wondered again if I could trust my own senses. "Maybe I should."

"Sometimes, a person is just guilty," she said. "No defense for that."

I nodded. When I was about halfway back to the car, Nguyen called her dog, and I realized the animal was following me. The dog looked back at Nguyen and then watched me drive away.

## CHAPTER 18

The elevator lifted me slowly to my floor in the hotel while I tried to come up with my next move. I tried to call Ben Chesniak, but he didn't answer. Before I could leave a voicemail, another call came through. It was Diane.

"Hey!" I said. "What's up? How are the dogs?"

She remained quiet for a moment. The elevator dinged, and I exited. Finally she said, "Not well, Jack."

"What do you mean?"

"Meega's not eating."

I slid my room key into the door and pushed it open. "She's still pissed about being taken to the pound and then me leaving town."

"It's more serious than that, Jack."

"What do you mean?"

"I took her to the vet. She has cancer."

"Cancer?" I repeated, still standing in the open doorway. "That's not possible. Dogs don't get cancer."

"Apparently they do, Jack. Canine hemangiosarcoma. We're giving her special food, but she's still not eating."

"What's the treatment? Do you need me to send money for medicine?"

"No, Jack. We're doing what we can to ease her pain, but… She's not eating because she is hurting, Jack. The vet says she won't make it more than a few weeks."

"Are you telling me Meega is dying?"

"The vet is recommending we put her to sleep."

I'd seen many animals die in the wild. We had lived free, but it was a harsh life. None of us had ever lived long enough to die of cancer.

"No," I said. "Maybe they got the lab results mixed up."

"Jack, she's in pain. She doesn't move. She doesn't eat."

I felt numb, but tears welled up in my eyes. "There must be a way." I waited, but Diane didn't respond. Even without words, her breath over the phone made me feel less alone. "I wouldn't be alive today if not for that dog. I owe her everything."

"I know."

She didn't know, of course. She couldn't understand how literal my words were. Meega had taught me how to survive. More than that, she and Alpha had sustained me with their companionship. Now that I was living the life of a man, I kept getting pulled away from the things that really mattered. My best friend and mentor suffered while I was here helping the man who had ruined my life.

"Don't do anything until I get there," I said. "Luis can handle things here." I didn't know how I would explain it to him. Luis didn't care about dogs. Hell, I don't think he cared about most people either, but Luis didn't matter right now. No matter what anyone said, I was going home.

I took in slow, shaky breaths and steadied myself against the doorframe. I had to get home, but my brain didn't want to function. What was step one? I checked my phone. It was after noon now. If I hurried, I could catch a late afternoon flight with one short stop and be home after dinner this evening. If I missed it, I'd be stuck here until tomorrow morning. I stuffed my belongings into my canvas bag. I had never fully unpacked anyway, so I didn't have much to grab. I just needed to squeeze it all in.

We were in a densely populated downtown, and three Uber cars were less than five minutes away. I decided to check out before requesting a car since they were so close. The elevator crawled along. The stairs would have been quicker.

A cute redheaded woman at the front desk beamed a friendly smile as though she didn't have a care in the world. "Was everything satisfactory?" She had no way of knowing my world was collapsing.

"Yes," I answered, "fine."

"I'm glad to hear that. We would really appreciate it if you could go online and leave a review."

"I'll think about it. Look, I'm in kind of a hurry."

"Oh, I'm sorry. Would you like a receipt?"

I didn't give a crap about receipts just then, but Luis would kill me if I didn't get one. "Yes, please."

"It will just take a moment."

My left fist tightened around the handles of my bags. I hadn't intended on standing here long enough to need to put them down. I set them beside me and opened the Uber app on my phone. The girl handed me the paper. I said, "Thanks," and clicked the last button on the app before heading out the revolving doors. A refreshing wind rushed around the downtown buildings and tousled my hair, helping ease my tension. It was cooler than I'd expected, and I was glad I'd brought my jacket.

A shiny black car immediately pulled up. A burly man in a white baseball cap called out the driver side window with a slight accent, possibly Eastern European. "Jack Mahler?"

"Kevin?" I said, saying the name on the ride sharing app. "That was quick!"

"Yes." He eyed my luggage. "You want me to pop trunk?"

I was already tossing my bags into the back seat. "No, that's fine."

The locks clicked automatically as he pulled away from the curb and raced around the city streets. I usually made conversation, but I was grateful not to have a chatty driver this time. I closed my eyes and let my head sink toward my lap.

My friend was suffering, had been suffering, and I had ignored it. She couldn't tell me what was wrong with words. I should have been more observant. I wondered if Meega realized how important she was to me. Once I was there, I could assess the situation firsthand, talk to the vet myself. Maybe there was something they had missed or hadn't communicated. I didn't want

Meega's last memories of me to be letting her get locked up and then leaving her.

Perhaps I was anthropomorphizing her too much. Dogs live in the now. It's quite liberating not to dwell on the past and agonize over future possibilities, but dogs do dream and relive the past when they sleep. They develop expectations based on previous experience. Canines remember their favorite humans when they aren't present. Dogs will circle their house looking for people who aren't there. We don't just cease to exist for them when we aren't in the room. Even I didn't know if dogs conceptualized humans as having positive and negative motivations or living extensive lives somewhere away from them, as I was currently doing. They understand actions and they want to be important to their pack. I hadn't been showing Meega how important she was.

My phone vibrated. I looked at my phone and found a message on the Uber app from Kevin, saying, *Where are you?*

The message confused me. I looked at the white baseball cap above the driver's seat and then at the trees lining the deserted little road. When had we left the interstate? The faded blacktop didn't even have a dividing line. Even through the closed windows I could smell pollen and swamp mud. I hadn't been paying attention and wasn't familiar with the city, but this didn't seem right.

"Hey, uh, *Kevin*," I called to the driver. "Is this the way to the airport?"

"Construction," the driver said. "We return to main road soon."

He looked back at me in the rearview mirror and I noticed the long scar on his right cheek. I inhaled the faint smell of outdoor sweat though my nose. This wasn't Kevin from the app. The app had listed a black Toyota Corolla. I thought I had seen a Toyota sign on this car, but I hadn't really looked. I must have been more distracted than I realized. This was my tail from the hotel lobby. What could Agent Wittman want with me now?

"I need to catch a plane." I let out an exasperated groan. "Tell agent Wittman I can talk to him another time."

The brows in the mirror furrowed in confusion, but the driver didn't say a thing.

"Am I under arrest?" I asked.

At that, the man's eyebrows raised and I caught the edges of a smile. That's when I realized there might be a reason this man didn't look like an FBI agent. But if he wasn't working for Wittman, who was he working for? The doors were stuck in the locked position, and I had no clue where we were. "Maybe I should call Wittman myself and get this worked out."

His eyes narrowed, becoming serious again. Without taking his eyes off me in the mirror, he pressed the accelerator to the floor, pushing me back into the seat. I opened up my recent calls on the phone, looking for Wittman's number, but then thought 911 might be more efficient. Before I could dial, the driver slammed on the breaks, squealing the tires. My head hit the seat in front of me, and the phone fell from my hand. My bag wedged itself between the backseat and the rear of the front passenger seat.

The car careened to a stop on the side of the road, leaving a trail of burning, black skid marks in its wake. The engine hummed softly as frogs croaked somewhere beyond the trees. The one time in two years that I really needed my gun was on the one case I didn't have it with me.

I felt the floor for my phone, but noticed my bag was still in motion. Everything else in the car had stopped moving, but something caused the canvas to bulge in and out. Instead of reaching for the phone, I zipped the bag half open and gasped. Brown, hairy fingers wriggled up and down. I shouted at the severed hand, "I don't have time to fight with you right now. I'm kind of busy at the moment!"

The driver's door swung open. I hadn't realized just how tall and broad-shouldered Fake Kevin was until he stood up. I guesstimated him at six foot eight and pushing 300 pounds. I forgot the severed hand and focused on the more immediate threat. *Kevin* held the rear door handle with one hand. He made sure I saw the big, blocky 9mm pistol in his other hand aimed at my head through the window. There was no way I could beat him in a straight on fight. If I didn't think of something, he'd leave me decomposing in the swamp, which had probably been his plan from the start. I wondered if this was the man who'd hacked off all those hands.

When the door opened, I plucked the wriggling hand from my bag and tossed it at the driver.

Dead fingers latched onto his arm. "What the hell?"

"You want hands so badly? Take that one!"

He shook his arm up and down. For a moment I thought the hand would be immediately dislodged, but it swung over the sleeve of his shirt and landed on his shoulder. His eyes bulged as he brushed at it frantically with both arms, turning completely away from me.

I launched myself out the door and into the man's legs. Already off balance, he went toppling backward. It is cliché but true— the bigger they are… Fake Kevin's head had a long way to fall. I was in the driver's seat before his white hat slammed the hard pavement.

The engine had been left running, and I slipped the car into gear. The tires screeched against the road. The pistol snapped, and the rear window cracked. I ducked as much as I could and weaved the steering wheel back and forth, not giving him a chance to aim at anything specific as bullets popped against the back and sides of the car. A couple shots clanged against the wheel well, but none of the tires appeared to take a hit.

Shots continued, but nothing more hit the car. I checked the rearview mirror and saw my would-be-killer, now shrinking with distance, shooting at the ground around him. I almost felt sad for the little, disembodied hand. At least now I knew I wasn't the only one who could see it. Not unless Fake Kevin was also part of my delusion.

I took a deep breath and tried to slow my breathing. I had no idea where I was and I appeared to be moving further out into the middle of nowhere. I didn't want to turn around for fear of running into Fake Kevin again. Rapidly moving clouds blew across the sky, so I couldn't even use the sun to get a basic sense of direction. It wasn't like me to let myself get so distracted. My phone was still somewhere on the floor in the back seat. Once I had a little more distance from the goon and felt a little safer, I could pull over and look for it.

I looked down on the console in front of me and spotted a glowing monitor on the dashboard. I toggled over to the GPS screen. A map showed an arrow, me, on a thin line, the only road in miles of swamp. Still moving the car away from my assassin, I flipped to a screen which read, *previous destinations*. On top of the list was the address of my hotel, and it was listed a few times. Only one other address repeated.

I finally pulled the car over to the side of the road and clicked on the repeated address. The GPS plotted a course and asked me to make a U-turn. If I kept going straight instead, there was a county road that would let me bypass Fake Kevin. In the glove box, I found rental car paperwork listed to a *John Smith*, most likely an alias. I glanced at the spider-webbed glass on the back windshield. He wouldn't be getting his security deposit back on this car. I wondered if he would report the car stolen, or just disappear.

The driver was obviously not with Wittman or the FBI. Assuming he wasn't some other random person who I had annoyed— there were many, but not here in Virginia— that meant *John Smith* was either involved with the stolen artifacts or the killings. My money was on the killings since he'd already shown himself willing to commit murder. But I wasn't anywhere near an answer on that case, and it wasn't even really my case in the first place, so why kill me? The other victims had been professors and scholars, while I had gone from high school straight into the military before getting kicked out.

My would-be assassin had politely left me a nearly full tank of gas. I'd already missed my plane, so I let the GPS lead the way.

The road remained a narrow strip of blacktop, but a dividing line appeared. Still water stagnated in ditches on both sides of the road. Twisted trees fell away to my left, and thick reeds sprouted as far as I could see. Telephone wires strung along wooden poles to my right. I'm not sure when I had crossed into North Carolina. In New Mexico, I could drive for hours before hitting another state.

GPS is a useful tool, but I found it less helpful than you might think. I turned onto a road and rounded a curve, coming upon a strip of family homes and neighborhoods.

The address I wanted didn't appear to exist. In the distance, a thin, white lighthouse, pinstriped in red like a candy cane, rose above the houses, and sand blew up against the buildings like snow drifts.

The GPS said I had passed my destination. I pulled into a driveway and turned back the way I had come. The house numbers here were similar to the one I wanted, but the road names didn't match and the exact number I needed never appeared. After turning around again, I pulled onto a dead end drive with no sign and put my car in park in front of a chain link gate, probably some kind of utility or beach access road. I found my phone under the seat and clicked on *Street View*. It pulled up the exact same panorama of beach houses I saw in real life.

I got out and wandered around the car. Salty air tousled my thinning hair and whipped my ponytail to one side. Clouds raced through the air. A door or shutter somewhere in the distance slammed back and forth in the wind. I put my hands in my jacket pockets and held the fabric close. Beyond the chain link gate, the blacktop drive transitioned to loose gravel.

A thick arm encircled my throat like an anaconda, and I gasped a breath of outdoor sweat. Blowing debris and shifting winds must have covered the goon's approach. I grabbed the bulky, muscular limb, but it remained cemented to my neck, and I felt a hand on the back of my head. I lowered my chin, using it and my hands in an attempt to push my attacker's arm away, but it wouldn't budge. I jabbed a hand and elbow behind me, grabbing at anything and everything I could reach. I kicked back at his legs and feet as I struggled, which in hindsight may have put more pressure on my neck, but what did I have to lose?

If he perfected the sleeper hold, he could simply hold me until the lack of blood to my brain killed me. If I'd seen him coming, even just a shadow of movement, I would have had a chance. I grabbed the arm holding me with both hands, lifted my legs in the air and twisted, shifting our center of gravity. The giant body holding me fell sideways, but my eyes were already seeing spots as we plummeted to the ground.

# CHAPTER 19

The hotel bed was colder and harder than I remembered, but the cold was oddly refreshing. I felt beneath me and realized I was lying on concrete. Mildew overpowered the smells of fish and sea salt.

A profile of Specialist Edward Morales came into focus sitting sideways on a cot against the opposite curved wall. "Why did you have to be so nosey?" he asked. "You had as much reason to hate Anderson as I did! More!"

I sat up and the blood rushed from my head. This was the third time I'd been rendered unconscious in less than a week. That couldn't be good for my health. I was lucky to still be alive. A single light bulb hung from a sloped ceiling, and a small, round window above our heads showed rapidly moving clouds.

"What reason did you have to hate him so much?" I asked. "I thought you were friends. He helped you get hired as a private contractor."

Morales scoffed, and I heard my own emphatic words from his mouth. "He is *not* my friend. There aren't any private jobs anymore, at least not for people like me. Not jobs that make bank like when Anderson got into the game." He paused and wiped his eye. "Anderson had everything handed to him— the golden boy and his loving mother."

"You knew his mom?"

"I visited the old lady a couple years ago, before I knew anything about any artifacts. I had to see where a turd like Anderson floated up from." He laughed. "She gave me cookies! My own mom never gives me shit. I slept that night in his storage unit, surrounded by his garbage."

"You're obsessed!"

"Maybe I was, but I've gotten my revenge. He's out of my system now."

"You managed to smuggle the antiquities into the country without getting caught. You could have sold them all and gotten rich. Why just shove them in someone else's storage unit?"

"Castor wasn't interested in anything but the bowl."

"Castor!" I exclaimed. "Jules Castor was your buyer?"

"Of course! I thought you knew. He paid me enough for that stupid bowl that I could retire young! I will never be anybody's bitch again. I wake up when I want to wake up and go to bed when I want to go to bed. I tried to sell the other artifacts, thinking I'd make an even bigger score, but every platform I looked at was traceable back to me. I didn't have any experience fencing stolen artifacts."

"If the money Castor already paid you just for the bowl was enough to set you up for life, you could have thrown the rest of the artifacts in the garbage or donated them anonymously. No one would have looked at you twice!"

"How could I waste such an opportunity? If all the platforms were traceable, why not let them be traced back to Anderson? It was perfect!"

"But that was such a huge risk after you'd already gotten away with it! Besides, Anderson didn't take those artifacts."

"He did plenty of other bad things and never got punished! This was karma, baby. He kept rising up, making more money, getting more women, while I get busted by Nguyen just 'cause I showed up for duty a little buzzed one time! From drinking alcohol I'd gotten from Anderson! The very same hooch Nguyen had been drinking with him the night before! But I'm the one to get in trouble!" He took a deep breath. "If he wasn't going to be caught for what he really did, I'd get him caught for something he didn't do. And even if he somehow skated by, everyone would finally hear about his other infractions. It was the perfect plan!"

"Not perfect if you get caught."

His upper lip curled into a sneer. "I'm not caught yet."

I nodded my head toward the door. "I assume that door is locked? You look just as trapped as me right now. Your buyer must not be too happy with all the attention you brought to this. With all the work you put into this scheme, you surely could have sold the other artifacts a lot easier than framing Anderson."

"Like you said, the money from just the bowl was enough to set me up for life. I didn't need more money. Anderson's downfall is worth more to me than a few million dollars."

"Oh, yeah, just a few million in pocket change. If you get caught, you can still retire to a nice prison."

Morales laughed. "I told you— I'm not caught yet."

I rested my head against the cool, curved drywall. The sound of Morales' voice wasn't helping my pounding head. The worst part of his story was realizing that I felt the same way he did. I wanted to see Anderson taken down. I wanted a vicarious revenge for what he had done to me all those years ago. Anderson seemed to always get away with everything while the people around him fell.

"How does one become a smuggler, exactly?" I asked. "If you didn't have any experience stealing antiquities, how did you end up involved in the first place?"

"Castor sent his guy to Iraq to find the missing bowl—"

"The white-haired goon with the gun?"

"That's him. The Coalition kicked him out of the country before he'd found what he was after, but I overheard the conversation and got his card. I just happened to know an Iraqi family who was safeguarding some artifacts. They planned to turn them back into the museum once the country was stable again. When I showed up in my uniform and offered to keep them safe, they gave them to me— just gave them to me! They didn't even ask for any money!"

The lock clicked and the door squeaked open. Harsh light from the hanging bulb reflected off Castor's polished head. He beckoned me with the Walther PPK in his hand. "So good to see you again, Mr. Mahler." The shiny little pistol had a marbled brown grip.

"I wish I could say the same. What are you up to, Castor?"

"Haven't you pieced it together yet? You are a fascinating individual, Mr. Mahler. I still don't know how you connected the dead academics and the missing artifacts."

Morales stood and glared at me. "No one else would have cared enough to keep looking! Anyone else would just let Anderson take the fall!"

The veins bulged in Castor's temples. "No one wants to hear from you, Morales. If not for you, Mahler wouldn't have started sniffing around in the first place!" Castor backed away from the exit to make room for me.

He thumbed the safety off as I brushed by, leaving me no room to fight. I had no doubt Castor would shoot me at the slightest provocation. The older style PPK's shot .32 caliber ammunition, the same type of bullets found in the handless victims.

Once I was out of the room and a few feet down the hall, Castor slammed the door on Morales and locked it.

Morales banged his fist on the door. "Come on! Let me out!"

"I'll deal with you later." Castor urged me forward, remaining far enough behind that I couldn't take him out before getting shot. "Morales has a point, though," Castor said. "No one else cares enough about Anderson to keep digging."

I winced. *Care* might be a bit of a strong word." I left the rest of his implication alone. With me out of the way, no one else was likely to believe a sleaze like Anderson could possibly be innocent.

In the outer room, Benaiah Chesniak sat at a dining table littered with thick books and yellowed papers. His thinning comb-over fell about his head in random bundles, and his reading glasses sat crooked on his nose. Fake Kevin leaned against a dark, wood-paneled wall with folded arms and watched over Ben. Stairs disappeared behind the curved wall at his back.

"Kevin!" I exclaimed. "You made it to the party! I hope you understand I'm going to have to give you a negative review on the ride sharing app."

He glowered at me but remained a man of few words.

"I trust you are ready, Rabbi," Castor said. "It is time."

Ben met my eyes and then looked at the gun in Castor's hand. "There was no need for this, Jules. I would have helped you for free, if you had asked. This is fascinating work. I don't understand the need for threats."

"We don't have time for fascinating work on your off hours, Rabbi. This needs to be done now!"

I scowled at our captor. "Fanatics don't need reasons."

Castor's brows lifted and he grinned maniacally. "Fanatic? I expected more from you, Mr. Mahler. You shall soon see how rational I am when this zeal pays off!"

Ben grabbed a notepaper, and Castor motioned for us to exit though an arched, wooden frame. Air from the open door blew books and pages from the table.

I assumed Castor meant to kill me, but then why take Ben with us, unless he meant to kill him too? Did that mean Castor had gotten whatever he had wanted from him?

"Where are you taking us?" I asked.

Wind whipped Castor's white suit jacket around his bulky frame. "Just for a little walk on the front lawn," Castor said. "I thought you might want to see the last ritual for yourself. You've earned that much, at least, Mr. Mahler. I really do like you. A curious mind is such a rarity."

A long, narrow drive split the ocean waves on a path back to the rocky shore. Rough water splashed the strip of earth. The fresh, salty breeze cleared my head. I looked back at the building behind us. The pinstriped lighthouse towered into the circling clouds above.

I turned to Ben and whispered as we marched. "What is this all about? What do they want from you?"

He shook his head and raised his brows. "He is insane! He merely wants me to read an inscription and the name of an old god. I have recordings of Aarif and the others saying the name, but Castor says they all got it wrong. I believe Aarif had the consonants right, but the vowels aren't obvious in Semitic—"

"That's enough," Castor said. "I don't care how you do it, just that you do it. It is time to put study into practice, Rabbi."

# CHAPTER 20

With water roiling on either side of us, we came upon the ancient, mottled brown bowl centered on the gravel drive. At over fifteen inches wide and seven inches tall, *bowl* didn't seem an adequate description. *Basin* might have been a better word. Its rim was over half an inch thick, making me think it might be heavier than it looked and certainly harder to smuggle into the country than some tiny rings.

I made eye contact with the dead man standing behind the bowl. Aarif Bulsara, or the thing wearing his face, wore a billowy pale tunic and gold belt. My eyes fell to his right hand, which was purple and splotchy at the wrist. I recognized the hand as the same one in my hotel room, but it had somehow found its way back and reattached itself. Perhaps it had hitched a ride back with Fake Kevin, or perhaps I was overthinking it, and ghostly hands didn't need transportation.

Castor spoke over the wind. "It is the perfect location, don't you think? Air, earth and water all coming together!"

"If you say so," I said.

Castor grinned. "I still don't understand, Mr. Mahler, what connected the artifacts to the killings? What led you down this path?"

No one else acknowledged Bulsara, and I wasn't sure if the others saw him or not. *He* was what had led me down this path. The spectre in the evidence room, the animated hand— without them, I never would have made it this far. They had led me to the truth, but also possibly to my death.

There was no reason to tell Castor all that, though. "Nothing led me here. Until your man kidnapped me, I had no evidence you were connected. I was on my way home and you would have gotten away with it."

Castor's nostrils flared as he studied me. "Oh, I am more than getting away with it! None of that will matter soon enough." He clicked on a digital audio recorder with one hand, and pointed the gun at Ben with the other.

The rabbi kneeled and dipped his ring finger into the ancient bowl. Through the clear water in the vessel, I could now make out darkened alien writing etched into the interior surface and spiraling all the way to the bottom. As Ben stirred the water with his finger, he mumbled in an ancient tongue. Bulsara, or the thing that looked like Bulsara, stood opposite Ben, eyes wide with intense anticipation. Ben's voice gained power as he continued. His words pulled at something deep inside me.

At last Ben paused, and his voice echoed. *"Ngimntsukal."*

The wind roared, and something broke loose within me. Waves of water crashed over the banks and shot into the sky overhead. The mysterious man I knew as Aarif Bulsara arched his back and swelled twice his height. Colorful wings swooped down from his back, creating a circle of calm in the cyclonic wind. Ivory feathers covered his neck and head like protective plates of armor, and a clawed foot gripped the ground.

Wide-eyed Ben definitely saw the creature now. His pupils dilated, and he shielded his face with his right hand as the monster's giant beak arced toward him.

I gasped, waiting for the spirit or demon or god, whatever it was, to gnash Ben's hand off as it had done to the others. Instead of striking, however, it dropped to one knee and closed its eyes in a low bow. Its beak nearly touched the gravel.

The pounding waves spouted high above our heads, but instead of crashing, the water sprayed like a series of fountains in crisscrossing arches over Ben's head. Sea birds circled above.

Castor laughed maniacally over the wind, and his goon gazed up nervously at the circling birds and arching fountains.

I fell forward as though pulled on a string, mimicking the movement of Bulsara. I landed on my hands, but my hands weren't hands anymore. My thumb moved up my arm. Hair sprouted over my limbs. Panic gripped my heart. The last time I had changed like this, I had been lost for nine years. I'd finally climbed my way back up into something resembling a real life again. I cried out to ask what was happening, but all that emerged was a gravelly whine. My throat couldn't make words anymore. I couldn't survive another nine years as an animal. I didn't have the strength to fight my way back again.

Through tearing eyes, I caught a glimpse of red beside me. Alice McGuiness, the woman from my last case, bowed with me in her red dress. I wanted to ask when and how she had arrived, but neither of us was capable of speech.

Bulsara's voice boomed in my head. "All hail King Benaiah Chesniak. Your wish, is our command."

I looked up to see Ben's mouth hanging open as he gazed down at the bowing god. A tiny smile crept across his face and his eyes swelled. He must have realized what this meant. *King Chesniak was no longer a prisoner.* Like Sargon thousands of years before him, Ben had recited the ancient name, and with it came the power of the gods.

Thunder snapped, and my back seized. I fell forward again as two more shots pierced the day. Wind sucked the smell of gunpowder from my nostrils even before Ben landed face down on the gravel. Blood stained the back of his shirt.

Ngimntsukal reeled his beaked head back from the sight of his wounded king. The arching fountains splashed against the earth and chilled my fur before draining back into the sea.

Crashing water knocked Fake Kevin to the ground. He looked at the bird god and then at me in wide-eyed terror. It was nice to know that some things scared even this giant goon. If my mouth had been human, I would have mocked him, but all I could do was bark. Alice was now gone, if she had ever really been there at all.

Castor lowered his gun and dove for the bowl.

I bared my teeth, wishing I had my own gun, but my paws would not have been able to fire it. I wriggled out of my pants as I raced forward on all fours. Every hair on my wet, furry body screamed for me to run away from the giant god and the circling winds, but I forced myself onward.

Castor inserted his finger into the mystic bowl. The first syllable of the ancient name was barely out of Castor's mouth when my teeth clamped down on his hand. He tried to pull away, and I jerked my head side to side, ignoring everything else around me. Castor screamed, and blood oozed around my jaws and tongue.

He clenched his eyes shut and, with a remarkable amount of control, shouted, "Ngimntsukal!"

I fell free and rolled across the gravel.

Castor cradled his hand and cackled madly as the wind howled. He looked to Ngimntsukal expectantly, but the god form was gone. Thin Aarif Bulsara motioned passively to the overturned bowl and spilled water. Castor frowned at the blood spurting from his hand.

I opened my mouth, and Castor's finger dropped into my now human hand. When the bowl had tipped over, it must have disrupted the magic ceremony, but now that Castor knew the secret name, he could simply try again.

Castor saw me eying the bowl and his gun next to it. He growled with more animalism than I'd had in my canine throat as he charged me.

He raced right into my swinging fist.

# CHAPTER 21

With his employer on the ground, Fake Kevin took off running down the drive to the chain link gate. I was relieved. There is no way I could take the goon down in a fair fight, and he most likely had a gun, but his fear of the supernatural must have gotten the better of him.

Ngimntsukal nodded at me. "I knew I spotted Enkidu within you. The vessel is now yours. You have but to right the bowl, say my name and have anything you desire."

I stared at the severed finger in my hand, and wondered if I could say the name correctly. I had heard it twice and was pretty sure I could get it close, but if one accent was in the wrong place, I'd lose my hand like the real Bulsara and the other dead scholars. The consonants felt unnatural in my English speaking mouth. Were the vowels *ewww* or *uuuu?* Trained linguists had failed, while I had stumbled over Captain Nguyen's name, one of the most common last names in today's world.

"Power," Ngimntsukal continued, "money, women, men. The limits are only your imagination."

"Okay, Nim Sucker, give me a minute!"

He reared back his head with wide eyes at my intentional bastardization of his oh-so-sacred name. In a thousand years, I bet no one had ever called him that.

I righted the heavy bowl and examined the letters etched into its surface. I'd struggled so hard, and what did I have to show for it? I still lived paycheck to paycheck. Now I held the power of a god in my hands. What would I do with that kind of power? I thought of poor Meega, then spotted Ben still lying on the ground. "Health?" I wondered aloud.

"You could live forever."

"Is that what you told King Sargon?"

I dropped the finger in the bowl and crouched next to Ben. He lay on his stomach with his head to the side. Sea water had watered down the pool of blood underneath him. I made sure his airway was clear. He had a rapid pulse, and his breathing came in quick, shallow bursts.

"Stay with me!" I said.

He blinked and looked at me with wide, terrified eyes— a good sign, but I wondered if it was death he was afraid of, or me. How much had he seen and understood? His skin was so cold and wet. I lifted his shirt. Not one, but three bullets had gone in. One had penetrated his right scapula, missing his heart by a few inches. Another pierced the left shoulder, while the last went through two ribs near his diaphragm.

A faint smile crossed the god's thin lips. "King Sargon revealed the secret of the bowl to one of his wives. She stole it thinking that would make her son king, but neither she nor her son could read or write. There was nothing more I could do for Sargon once he lost my bowl."

I blotted Ben's wounds with his shirt. The first two shots had clotted pretty well, but the lower one still seeped blood. I pressed his shirt against it. "And what about Ben?"

The corners of Ngimntsukal's mouth sank downward. "King Benaiah Chesniak had but to ask, and I could have saved him. I so wanted him to ask. He would have been a noble king."

"You can still help him!" I shouted. "It was you who sent me down this road. You have the power!"

"I am not powerless, but I am limited. The true power belongs to the spirits of the material world around us. They only obey me when I have the King's authority to command them."

"If you wanted my help, you should have just told me what was going on! I could have stopped it! Ben didn't have to get hurt!"

"There are rules I must follow." He knelt with me and stroked Ben's head. He gazed upon Ben's face as he had the sculpted head of Sargon in the FBI property room.

I didn't quite understand, but Ngimntsukal kept talking, and I wasn't about to stop him if he was finally feeling chatty.

"I knew the first time Castor woke me that he would not be a good king. He thought nothing about cheating the gods' rules. A world with him in control would not have been pleasant. I would have done many distasteful things in his name. But his meddling allowed me time to explore this strange new era. Things are so different than when last I awoke…" He shook his head. "But humans have not changed."

I lifted the shirt from Ben's wound. Constricted blood vessels had slowed the bleeding. He'd gone into shock. I'd normally flip him over and elevate the legs, but that could cause him to bleed out quicker. I covered him with my jacket to help him retain warmth. He wouldn't last long without help, and I'd done all I could. My mind drifted again to poor Meega suffering back home without me.

"Hang on, Ben!" I shouted, but I was unsure if he could understand me. "I'll get help!" His eyes were closed again.

"What about health for someone else?" I asked the strange deity. "Is that something you can give?"

"You have but to say my name, Jack Mahler."

I stood. "And if I say your name wrong?"

His eyes drifted down my side. "You know that rule."

I looked at my right hand— a human hand, thankfully. Without Castor to shoot me in the back, I might survive having it ripped off. Would it be worth the risk?

I found my pants, but my cell phone wasn't in the pocket. "My only wish is that Castor and Morales be tried for their crimes."

Ngimntsukal raised his eyebrows. "Are you sure?"

I paused, looking at the severed finger in the bowl. "It's too much power for any one person."

A broad smile filled the god's borrowed face. "You are wise, Jack Mahler."

"First time anyone's called me that. Probably the last, too."

I searched Castor's jacket pockets and found his phone. He began to struggle, so I drove my knee into his back and used his suit jacket to tie his wrists behind him. It wouldn't hold long, but would work until I found something better.

His phone had one of those features that unlocked when I held it up to Castor's face, even with the broken nose, and I was able to dial 911.

I turned back to Ngimntsukal. "Is there any way to prevent this from happening again?"

Ngimntsukal nodded. "Simply obscure the inscription."

"That's it?"

"With no name, there is no me."

"No you— What does that mean? Will you die?"

"The vessel is the only thing binding me to this world. When I go, I… I suppose it is a kind of death."

I hesitated.

"I have been trapped in that bowl a long time, Jack Mahler. That is not living. This will not end as long as the inscription remains. Now that the secret is known, someone else will come for the bowl, and they may not be as short-sighted as these petty criminals."

I found a rusty nail on the ground and started grinding away at the inscription inside the bowl.

"You don't need to destroy every letter. Merely make my name unreadable."

Castor rolled over and tried to stand, but having his wrists bound slowed him down. "Don't waste all that power, Jack! If you won't do it, let me say the name! I can heal Chesniak! I can share the power! The world is a big place! We can rule it together!"

As he was about to rise to his feet, I hefted the bowl up and swung the base into Castor's face. It rang with a satisfying thump, and he toppled over. I sat back down and continued scratching through alien letters.

Ngimntsukal nodded and smiled. "You are wise indeed, Jack Mahler." He turned and walked away.

I paused, saying, "Thank you, Nim-zu-kal."

On hearing his name, the god turned and cocked his head. "Not bad, Jack Mahler."

I stopped etching. "You mean—"

"The accent was a bit off on the second syllable. You made the correct choice."

I smiled and nodded. My arm was getting tired, so I switched hands, continuing to grind away at the ancient script. "How did you get stuck to this bowl in the first place?"

He didn't respond, and when I looked up, he collapsed into a thin dust of smoky, rose-scented sand.

# CHAPTER 22

I waved my hand, rejecting the bourbon Weinstein offered. Luis and Anderson clinked glasses in the conference room at Weinstein's office. I didn't feel much like celebrating and certainly not with Anderson. Ben was out of critical condition, but I was too embarrassed to visit him. How much had he seen while he lay there bleeding? How much did he understand? Had he witnessed my transformation? Would he ask me to explain? I couldn't face him.

Anderson raised his glass. "I knew I did the right thing by hiring you, Jack!"

"By hiring Navarro Investigations," Luis corrected.

I wondered aloud, "There is still a missing piece to this puzzle. Who was the money?"

"What do you mean?" Anderson asked.

"Castor funneled a lot of money back and forth in his auction business, but it was other people's money. He didn't have a million dollars on hand to pay Morales."

"That's the FBI's problem," Weinstein said.

Luis nodded. "We proved Anderson didn't do it. Our job is done."

I looked to my former sergeant. "But with your secrets out, your life will never be the same."

Anderson shrugged and sipped from his glass. "That's okay. I've got a bit of money saved up. I was thinking about retiring anyway, finally settling down. Maybe I'll write my memoires."

I shook my head. "Retiring before you even hit fifty years old? Karma never seems to touch you, does it?"

"That's why I wanted you, Jack. You always do the right thing, even when you don't want to."

I felt my jaw tighten. "Do I?"

My hand clenched. I imagined my fist jolting forward and Anderson's smug jaw crunching under my knuckles. I most likely would have gotten away with it. Anderson wouldn't press charges. He owed me that much. But I remembered the photo of us at his mom's apartment and found myself suddenly feeling sorry for him. I turned away and closed the door on this chapter of my life.

\* \* \*

Reece inserted his stick into the campfire and almost immediately shouted, pulling out the flaming marshmallow. I blew out the flames and examined the charred treat. "Perfect!" I said.

Reece poked at the blackened, bubbled shell. I sandwiched it with a chocolate brick between two graham crackers, slid it off the stick and handed it to the boy. He opened his mouth wide.

I cautioned, "You might want to let it cool a bit first."

I lifted the chocolate away from Alpha's curious nose and gave him half a hot dog instead. I gave the other half to Meega, who lay beside Reece's camping chair in the flickering light. Meega thumped her tail once and gnashed the meat into mush. Alpha sniffed at the larger dog's mouth and looked to me expectantly. His own treat had been gobbled down in seconds and was already a fading memory. Alpha always ate quicker than Meega, even in the best of times. Meega was still sick. Still dying. But the meds and special diet had made her comfortable. I was so grateful to have this time with her.

This was not like the camping trips the dogs and I had taken before. This was better. We'd brought chairs and a tent and food for Reece's benefit, which I had assumed would spoil the experience, but I was enjoying it way more than I had expected. The dogs certainly liked it better too. None of us were pups anymore, and roughing it was hard on our old bodies. A few creature comforts were more pleasant than sleeping in the grass or failing to catch our own food.

While we were up here in the Sandia Mountains, Diane and Luis could have an evening to themselves.

I kept my marshmallow a few inches from the flames and let it cook more slowly than Reece's had.

Reece watched me. "Can I have another?"

"Of course! Have at it!"

He waited, still watching me. I think he expected me to prep it for him again. Maybe it never occurred to him that he could do it for himself.

"You don't need to wait for me," I said. "Go ahead."

Meega stiffened, and a low growl resonated within her chest. Alpha planted his feet and yipped at the surrounding forest.

"What is it?" Reece asked.

I stared into the shadows beyond the trees. "Probably just a raccoon." I said it quietly, not quite believing my own words. The dogs might bark and wag their tail at a raccoon, but they seemed agitated.

A man in a black suit strolled out of the darkness, and Alpha hid between Reece's chair and Meega. Putrid incense clung to the man's suit jacket.

Reece startled, but greeted the stranger. "Hello."

I narrowed my eyes. It was rare to run into a fellow camper this far into the mountains at this time of night, but not impossible. This guy wasn't dressed for camping, however, and no one had ever gotten this close to my camp without me sensing they were coming. Perhaps the lack of a tie was his way of roughing it. Leathery skin hung from high cheek bones. Receding grey hair parted at the side, and round wire-rimmed glasses perched on a long, slender nose.

His syllables lingered in the air like a slithering snake. "You are a difficult man to find, Mr. Mahler."

Hearing my name sent a chill through me. Even if someone knew I was here, there was no way they should have been able to find my specific camp on an entire mountain filled with potential

# AN AUTHOR'S NOTE

In *Waking Terror* I talked about meeting the real life Jack Mahler (not his real name), and getting permission to write his stories.

When I received my finalized *Waking Terror* books in the mail, I was so excited to send off Jack's contributor copies. I didn't warn him they were coming. I wanted him to be surprised. I expected he would call as soon as he received them, as thrilled as I was to see his story in print.

A few days passed with no word. I kept waiting, thinking he must be busy or that maybe there was a delay in the mail. An additional week passed, and I became concerned that perhaps he wasn't responding because he didn't *like* what I had done to his story. This was supposedly his actual life, after all, even if I had my doubts as to how much of it really happened the way he claimed. Maybe he didn't appreciate the minor liberties I had taken in the name of artistic license and improved story structure. Or perhaps this just wasn't as big a deal to him as it had been for me.

I finally called him and left a voicemail… "Just wanted to make sure you got the books. Hope you like them. Call me."

I gave him another couple days to get back with me. I didn't want to be a bother, but my official book launch loomed closer, and releasing the book to the public before hearing from him felt wrong. I finally called again and left three more voicemails.

I had no choice but to do the book release without talking to him first. Now I became concerned for his safety as well and left more voicemails. He'd been so responsive during the writing process. It wasn't like him to ignore me.

I'd been keeping Jack's notebooks on the passenger seat of my car so that whenever I had a break, I could read over his case notes and make notations to myself for future books. After an event in Fountain Square, I found my passenger side window broken. The only things stolen from my car were Jack's notebooks.

I managed to get hold of his friend and colleague, Diane Bowen (also not her real name). She said she hadn't seen or heard from Jack in over a month!

I am forced to conclude Jack is in some kind of trouble. I hope he is safe, wherever he is.

Jack, I hope you find this book on a shelf someday and like what you see. If you are reading this, know that your friends are worried about you.

# ABOUT THE AUTHOR

**Matthew Barron** spends his days mixing and analyzing human blood as a medical technologist in Indianapolis, Indiana. Matthew's diverse fiction has appeared in magazines and anthologies such as *Ill-Considered Expeditions, Roboterotica, Outposts of Beyond, Sci Phi Journal, House of Horror* and more. He's produced two of his plays and released three graphic novels: *Temple of Secrets, The Brute* and *Harmony Unbound*. His sword sorcery book, *Valora*; dystopian novella, *Secular City Limits*; and kids book, *The Lonely Princess* are also available.

Photo by Liz A. Thomson

For more information, visit
matthewbarron.com
or
submatterpress.com

# EXPERIENCE WAKING TERROR, JACK MAHLER'S DEBUT

A nightmare haunts the Albuquerque suburbs.

PI Jack Mahler thought he finally had an easy assignment, a routine life insurance claim investigation. He was looking forward to having the afternoon off to go hiking with his dogs, but the widowed husband acts like he has something to hide, and Jack witnesses a surreal apparition feeding on the dead wife's ghost. When the voiceless entity follows Jack home and a rogue policeman threatens to frame him for murder, this easy case gets personal. To solve this mystery, Jack must seek answers in his own shameful past, risking life and sanity to discover the secret of the waking terror before his dream of a normal life turns to smoke.

Why can't anything be simple?

SUBMATTERPRESS.COM

# THE WORLDS OF MATTHEW BARRON

## DYSTOPIAN

## FANTASY

## KID'S FICTION

## GRAPHIC NOVELS

## AND MORE

AVAILABLE FROM

**SUBMATTER PRESS**

SUBMATTERPRESS.COM

Made in the USA
Monee, IL
23 August 2021